ADORABLE FAT GIRL ON SAFARI

Bernice Bloom

CHAPTER ONE

I should have known that it was the most ridiculous idea in the world. It had 'bonkers' written all over it from the start. Going off on safari with a woman I didn't know? What was I thinking? It was weapons-grade madness. But somehow it didn't seem like that at the time. Certainly, I had no idea as I sat there on that chilly March evening that things would get so out of hand. I had no inkling at all that, by the end of the month, I'd be on a continent far away, stuck up a tree in my knickers with a couple of screaming baboons while gun-toting rangers rushed to the scene. Nor did I realise that the video of my whole embarrassing episode would end up trending on Twitter. But - let's not get ahead of ourselves - we'll get onto all that. First, let me take you right back to the beginning...

It began on a cool winter's evening with a phone call completely out of the blue.

"It's Dawn Walters here," said a voice. "Remember me - we bumped into each other in the garden centre last week. I know you from school."

"Of course," I said. I remembered her very clearly from Rydens High School - this huge, jovial, loud, larger-than-life girl who everyone liked, but no-one wanted on their netball team.

"How are you?" I asked. I had no idea why she was phoning. She'd been very friendly when we'd bumped into one another in the centre. I work there as a supervisor and she'd come in looking through the outdoor plants for something to give to her mum on her birthday. Her great friendliness towards me was motivated, I suspected, by her delight at seeing how much weight I'd put on since we last saw one another. I was always so skinny at school, she probably assumed I'd gone from a skinny-legged child to elegant, size eight woman...then we'd locked eyes over the potted plants 12 years later, and she'd realised the girl who once weighed eight stone was now around 19 stone.

"You've changed," she'd said, almost delirious with joy. "I mean - you've really changed."

"You're just the same," I'd retorted. She was about 18 stone at school and was now about 25 stone, so I was being generous.

We'd exchanged numbers and muttered something about keeping in touch, must go for coffee, lovely to see you, and that was that; I hadn't really expected her to call. To be honest, I'd thrown away the scrap of paper with her number on it. I'd just thought we were being polite when we promised to keep in touch. But Dawn had followed through. Not only that, but she had a peculiar proposition for me.

"Look – this might sound odd, but do you want to come to Sanbona with me? It's a safari in South Africa?" she said.

I sat there in silence, realising I must have misheard her, but not quite sure what she actually said.

"Are you still there, Mary?"

"Yes," I replied. "I didn't quite catch what you said though."

"I know it's mad, but I just wondered whether you fancied a free trip to South Africa...with me...to, you know, see animals and stuff."

"Um. Gosh, yes," I replied, still not sure that I could have heard her correctly. I mean...who would do that? Who would invite someone on holiday when they hardly knew them. "When is the holiday?" I asked. "What will we do? How will we get there? Um – why are you inviting me?"

"I get free trips. I told you – I'm a blogger these days. I write a travel blog called 'Fat & Fearless' and I get invited to experience holidays and write about them."

"Yes, I remember," I said. "It all sounds amazing but why would you want me to come? I mean – we don't know each other, except from Mrs Thunder's French class, and that was over a decade ago."

"I get invited to loads of places, and I try to invite different people to come with me every time. I just thought you might fancy it?"

"Yes. That would be amazing. Of course I fancy it, I'd love to come. If you're sure?" I said.

"I'm positive."

"Great then," I said. "Great. I'll definitely come. Tell me a bit more about it."

"Well, it's a safari so it's – like – full of animals."

"What sort of animals?"

"Hang on, let me just look it up," said Dawn, and I could hear her tapping away on the keys while I waited, wondering what my boyfriend Ted would say when I told him. To be honest, we hadn't been getting on very well recently, so he'd probably welcome the break. We didn't live together but we spent a lot of time at one another's flats. Both of us would benefit from spending time apart rather than continuing to see one another every night when we both knew that things weren't right.

"There are lions, giraffes, cheetahs, oooo, look - elephants," she said.

"Elephants? How cool! Can we ride them?" I asked. I don't know why I said that...I guess I didn't know how to conduct a conversation about elephants.

"No, Mary, we can't ride them. Have you seen me? I'm 25 stones. My car struggles to move with me in it, I wouldn't subject an animal to that sort of brutality."

"Fair point," I said, thinking of the terrible groan that my suspension offered up every time I got into the driver's seat. Dawn was about six stone heavier than me, so I imagined her suspension must really have screamed every time she got in. Six stone! That was almost a whole person. Dawn was taller, wider and heavier than me. I felt petite next to her. I'd not felt petite next to anyone for about 15 years. I used to be a bit scared of her when we were at school...forever fearful that she might fall on me and crush me. Now I just thought it was nice that there was someone out there who was bigger than me.

"Look at their website," said Dawn. "The wildlife park is in the Karoo outside Cape Town, it's called Sanbona. That's S-a-n-b-o-n-a Wildlife Reserve. Take a look, it's bloody lovely."

I called up the pages as I chatted to Dawn. "Bloody hell!" I said, it looked like an incredible place. "There are lions, cheetahs, hippos and rhinos," it declared, showing them moving across the screen under the warm African sun. Birds swooped through the cloudless skies, as panpipes played. If the reality of the place was anything like as captivating as the marketing films on the website, it would be sensational. "We also have leopards, giraffes, zebras and elephants," I read. It looked bloody great.

"This place looks amazing," I said, clicking onto the section called 'our people'.

"Really, Dawn, it's amaz..." I stopped short as a picture flickered across the screen. Not a wonderful animal, but an achingly beautiful man... dressed in khaki and clutching a rifle. It was one of the rangers who'd be looking after us on our trip. He smiled slowly at the camera; a vision of masculine beauty in a branded baseball cap.

"Dawn, get onto the 'our people' section now," I cried, my voices several pitches higher than usual. "I'm not joking. Go on there now. Take a look at the bloody wildlife they've got there. This one's called Pieter. He's based at Gondwana Lodge. Please tell me that's the lodge that we're going to. He's perfect."

"Oh Good God Alive," said Dawn, reaching the short video on the website. "Oh hell, he's lovely. Wow. You know what, Mary Brown - we are going to have the best week of our lives."

CHAPTER TWO

Excitement about my impending trip carried me through the next few weeks. I booked the time off work and gleefully told everyone where I was going. Those I get on well with were chuffed to hear of my good luck, and those I don't care much for wrinkled their noses in distaste and pretended that they wouldn't give their right arm to be going on such a trip.

Ted was decidedly unimpressed by it all, certainly he didn't seem in the least bit bothered about me going to the other side of the world without him.

"I'm so stressed at work, babe," he'd said. "You know - there's loads going on and I need to get my head down and really get a handle on it all if I'm going to make salesman of the year again. The financial year ends in a month...I'm up to my neck You go, have loads of fun and I'll see you when you're back. OK?"

"Yes," I said, both relieved that he seemed so fine about me going away without him, and really unnerved that he seemed so fine about me going away without him. Couldn't he just have pretended to have been bothered? Couldn't he have pulled a pretend sad face and said how much he'd miss me?

Mum was mainly just confused by the whole thing, and I admit that I completely understood her confusion. I was still none-the-wiser about why Dawn had asked me rather than anyone else in the whole world. Don't get me wrong – it was incredibly lovely to be asked on the trip of a lifetime by a virtual stranger, but it was also really fucking odd.

"Dawn?" queried mum. "I don't think I've met her, have I?"

"I was at school with her. Her mum was a dinner lady and her dad had an affair with her aunty."

"Oh yes," said mum. It's coming back. Fat Dawn?"

"Yes," I replied, wishing mum hadn't called her that. I suppose it felt fine to call her Fat Dawn when I wasn't fat, but it felt far too close to home to call her that now.

"Blimey. Is she still as fat?" asked mum.

"She is," I confirmed.

"Well, you better make sure you don't ride any elephants then...you'll break them," she said

"I promise we won't ride any elephants," I told her. What was it with our family and riding bloody elephants?

"And behave yourselves – don't go getting drunk and silly like you do every time you go anywhere with that Charlie...I know what you two are like. Every time you two go anywhere it turns into a scene from The Hangover."

"Indeed," I agreed, and it struck me, not for the first time, that I had no idea what it would be like to go away with Dawn. I knew nothing about her. Would she be any fun? Perhaps she was a lesbian? Oh My God. Had I done the right thing? This could all go so horribly wrong.

"Send me pictures of tigers, won't you," mum said, while I was still panicking and running through scenarios in my mind where we were deep in the Karoo and Dawn made a move on me.

"Yes," I promised her. "I'll definitely send pictures of tigers."

"And I'll read the blog every day so I can keep up with what you're doing."

I made a mental note to tell Dawn to keep the blog as clean as possible. I'd looked through it several times since she'd asked me to go on safari and - I have to say - it was really very good. Quite witty and professional-looking, full of pictures, dry comments and clever observations. She'd obviously done a lot of travelling over the years, so the site was brimming with colourful tales from across the globe. It was also quite filthy. She didn't hold back on the swearing, and she wasn't averse to telling the world when she fancied someone...and what she might do to them if she got close enough.

Leaving day came round very quickly after the initial shock of the phonecall. I'd had the immediate panic about Dawn being a predatory lesbian, then the panic that I had nothing in my wardrobe that was in any way suitable for safari life. The latter of these two issues was easily solved with some light shopping in Marks and Spencers. Prior to my clothes buying expedition I'd read lots about safari life and watched films about colonial Africa. I had even printed off pictures detailing elegant safari wear. I'd bought the items I thought would be most suitable for the trip and packed them all carefully.

Now it was time to go, and I found myself standing by the front door of my flat, mentally running through everything I should be taking with me.

"Passport, ticket, safari clothing, toiletries," I said to myself. Was there anything else? I was paranoid that I'd forget something. I rummaged through my case one last time. Yes – all good. I must stop worrying.

All I needed to do now was to get to the airport, picking up Dawn from her flat in Esher en route. I'd promised that I would pay for the cab; it seemed like the least I could do when she'd organised a whole bloody holiday for me. To make the journey as hassle-free as possible, I'd downloaded the Uber app onto my phone.

We needed the cab for 4pm and it was around 3.45pm, so I put the destination details into the phone and waited for the car to show up. It told me that Ranjit Singh was nine minutes away in his Vauxhall Corsa. I was wearing my comfortable leisure wear, ideal for long haul travelling. My outfit was in a muted, fudge colour. I hadn't gone for bright colours, having felt such a fool the last time I went on holiday. I had a very comfortable pink onesie which I wore when I went to Amsterdam last year but I spent the whole time feeling like an overgrown toddler, or a Care Bear or something. This time I wanted to ooze style and sophistication

I checked in my bag for my passport one last time; then the phone bleeped to tell me that the car was outside, so I dragged my luggage out of the flat, bouncing it down the steps and making such a racket that Dave, my drop-dead gorgeous neighbour, came out of his flat downstairs to investigate.

"Going somewhere?" he asked.

"No Dave, I just like taking all my possessions with me   wherever   I   go."

"Ha, ha," he said, unimpressed by my witty repartee. "Where are you off to?"

"South Africa," I said.

"What are you going there for?" he replied.

"To see herds of elephants!"

"Of course I've heard of elephants," he replied. "What do you think I am? Some sort of dimwit?"

"No - a herd of elephants - like a flock of seagulls or a litter of puppies."

Honestly, it was like talking to a 90-year-old dementia patient sometimes. I can't believe I used to fancy this guy like mad, now I just feel half sorry for him and half maternal towards him.

"Oh. Herd of elephants! Yes," he said, as I bumped my bag to the side of the steps and brought it to rest. Not once did he move to help me, he just seemed to be looking off into the distance. "The babies are lovely."

"Babies?"

"Baby elephants," he said. "Real cute."

"Yes," I agreed.

"Want a hand with that, by the way?" Dave raised his eyebrows and pointed in the direction of my case.

"I'm good, thanks," I said, as I looked up and down the street for the uber driver. I couldn't see a car with just a driver sitting in it anywhere. The only car I could see had loads of blokes in it.

I went back onto the app to check. It seemed like the right car, in terms of its colour, but I couldn't see its registration. It couldn't be right though; it was full of people.

I stood on the kerb as Dave watched me, for some reason he seemed entranced and amused by the fact that I was going on holiday.

The car was close enough for me to see that it was definitely the right one; same registration number as the little car moving along the map on my phone. Presumably the men in there were about to get out.

I put my hand out to indicate my presence to the driver and he waved and pulled over.

"Hi," I said, and the three men in the car said 'hi,' back. None of them moved.

"Are you for me?" I asked. "I'm Mary Brown."

The driver nodded and jumped out of the car to help me put my bag into the boot. "Join the party," he said.

"Right," I replied, cautiously. There were three passengers on board – a large builder called Terry (who, it would turn out, knew everything in the world about sumo wrestling), a window cleaner called Ray who had his bucket and mops with him (his wife left him last week after 40 years of marriage but he never missed one window cleaning job), and a very large painter and decorator in his overalls, called Andy, who didn't talk much but snorted a great deal.

I squeezed into the back next to them. This was odd, but it was my first Uber. Perhaps this was how they worked? Little mini buses.

"We need to pick up my friend Dawn," I said, as the car trundled along, straining beneath the weight of us all. I waved at Dave who stared back, confusion written all over his face.

"This friend of yours…" said the driver. "She is small, isn't she? There's not a lot of room for anyone else."

I didn't answer. And so we sat there, me in my smart leisure wear with my handbag and travel documents perched on my lap while Terry demonstrated how he could talk in Japanese.

We were later than planned arriving at Dawn's house, so I phoned from my position cramped in the corner at the back of the car to apologise and say that I was on the way.

"Sure, heading out now," she said.

As long as I live I will never forget the look on her face when she saw this tiny, overburdened car screech up outside, with me squashed into the back of it next to the large men. The painter climbed out along with the window cleaner, dropping his mops as he went, then the builder from the front, still snorting.

"In you get," I said. I tried not to look at the driver's face. Dawn was dressed in tight green trousers and t shirt and looked way fatter than I remembered.

"What the hell?" she said, easing herself into the front seat next to the driver, while the builder climbed into the back. "Why do we have a bunch of construction workers in the back of the cab? We're just a red Indian short of a Village People tribute band. I can't arrive at the airport like this..."

"Konnichiwa." said Terry in his finest Japanese.

Ray scratched himself, Andy flicked through his phone looking at pictures of his recently departed wife and sighed occasionally and the car trundled along through the afternoon traffic, dropping off people along the way, en route to Heathrow Airport.

"What was that all about?" asked Dawn, as we took our bags from the boot and bid farewell to the driver.

"I don't know," I said. "I've never used uber before. I wasn't expecting there to be people already in the car."

"Show me what you did," instructed Dawn, taking my phone out of my hand.

I showed her the app, and how I'd just pressed the button for an Uber and put in the destination details. It was quite straightforward, even I couldn't have cocked this up.

"That's a bloody Uberpool car. You need to press this button," she said.

"Ohhhh..." I replied. "And what's an Uber pool car?"

"It's like a bloody mini bus, for God's sake. Uber pool cars are for people who can't afford Ubers. They are for poor people. Don't ever tell anyone what happened, will you," she said. "I can't have people thinking I travel in uberpool cars with random builders. I won't put it in the blog and let's not ever speak of it again."

"Sure," I said, as Dawn wandered off towards the terminal, leaving me with all the bags. I wondered idly, and with a certain degree of concern, whether I was about to go on a long haul flight and the holiday of a lifetime with the world's dullest person.

CHAPTER THREE

In the end I didn't sit next to Dawn on the flight...would you like to know why? Because Dawn made the most astonishing fuss and got herself upgraded to business. At no stage during the incredible fuss did she suggest that I might be upgraded as well. So I was stuck in economy, wedged between the window and a man and his wife who could not have looked less happy to be sitting next to me if I'd been carrying a bomb.

I do understand that it's a pain when someone is big and takes up more than their share of the room on a plane but – really – the snide looks and aggressive posturing weren't going to make me thinner, were they? They just made me feel desperately uncomfortable and ruined my whole journey. The rudeness also made me sad so I ate every morsel of food that was given to me to make myself feel better.

As I tucked into some terrible knitted chicken and plastic pasta I could see the two of them whispering and I just knew that they were talking about me and what terrible bad luck that they were next to a fatty, and how appalling that I was eating. Eating! How dare I?

I pulled my book out of my bag and read it aggressively. Can you read aggressively? Well, if you can – that's what I did. Although it wasn't so much reading as staring at the page and letting the words swim in front of my eyes while I tried valiantly to ignore the hostility brewing next to me. They would surely tire of feeling sorry for themselves sometime between now and South Africa, hopefully before we left European airspace, then we could all just relax, watch films, eat the terrible food and arrive in Cape Town without me strangling either of them.

I didn't sleep much on the flight because of Mr and Mrs Angry next to me and when we arrived in Cape Town airport I was exhausted. My tiredness wasn't helped by hearing all about Dawn's magnificent business class experience.

"It was quite wonderful," she said, then began reading out loud what she'd written about it for her blog. The way she wrote about the champagne, the characters, the lovely beds and nutritious food was really good. I mean – the whole thing made me feel jealous because I'd had such a horrible journey, but the writing was really classy. She might be an inconsiderate friend and a self opinionated oaf at times, but I could see why people wanted to read her blog, she wrote with humour and warmth that was quite compelling. In the piece she'd written how she was looking forward to our gentle meander down through the spectacular African countryside to the game reserve. She'd made it sound fantastic, and I was cheered by the prospect of the picturesque journey despite my tiredness.

"Will it be a nice car for the trip to the safari?" I asked, charitably setting her up with the opportunity to tell me how special she was and how companies would always send the best.

"It'll be a lovely limousine," said Dawn. "I'm quite a big deal in the blogging world, so they always send the best."

"Excellent" I said. "This is really exciting, isn't it?"

"It is, actually," she agreed. "I've never been on safari before. I hope I've brought the right clothes with me."

"I watched some films about Africa for inspiration," I said.

"Me too," said Dawn. "Out of Africa was beautiful."

"God, yes, amazing," I agreed.

Dawn called the limousine company while we were chatting, to ask about the car. There was certainly no sign of a plush limousine or a driver in a peaked cap.

"A what?" Dawn said, turning away from me and pacing around. She wandered off towards the money exchange places and hire car booths, articulating wildly with her hands as she went. I could hear her raised voice, but not the words she was saying.

All of a sudden she spun round and walked towards me, grabbing the handle of her wheelie case and shouting "follow me", I grabbed my bag and ran after her as the two of us waddled across the concourse and out onto the street.

"You need to know that this is not the way I normally travel, but there's been a cock up," she said, scanning the road for our transport to the Safari.

"Here it is," she said. "Oh my God, it's worse than I thought..."

Juddering to stop just next to us came an ancient Nissan Micra. It was small and dilapidated looking and covered in dust. The driver looked about 14.

"Oh my goodness, two big ladies for my car," he said in a rather ungentlemanly fashion.

"How far is it to Sanbona," I asked Dawn.

"About three hours," she said. "This is a disaster."

21

I couldn't be sure the suspension on this damn thing would cope with the combined weight of Dawn and me for three hours.

"A complete disaster," repeated Dawn.

It wasn't a complete disaster of course. Dawn had a habit of making everything that happened into a drama, but it wasn't the best of times - I'd had absolutely no sleep on the plane because I was cramped in economy next to anti-fattists, and now we'd emerged into the blazing heat to discover a dilapidated old car with no air conditioning was to take us down to Sanbona...which was three hours away. The plastic seats were already hot when we slid onto them. The temperature reading hovered around the 40*C mark. It was going to be the most sticky and unpleasant journey imaginable, and I was going to have to endure it all while sitting next to Dawn. There was no point in being miserable though - I decided the mood needed lifting a little.

"It's not a complete disaster," I said. "I've got a couple of those little bottles of wine from the plane in my bag. We can stop for refreshments if it all gets too much. Come on we can do this."

I reached into my bag and handed her a warm bottle of Sauvignon Blanc. "Thanks," she said, giving me the first smile I'd seen that day.

"Cheers," I said as we clinked the bottles together. I saw the driver shaking his head at us in the mirror. Had he never seen two enormous women drinking at 6am before?

The wine soon worked its magic and we glanced at each other as the car flew over yet another bump on the ancient roads. "This is fucking ridiculous," said Dawn.

"Yep," I said in agreement as we sat there sweating and laughing as the sun beamed down on the little car driving through the Karoo.

The journey that was supposed to take three hours ended up taking closer to five, in the dilapidated old excuse for a car.

By the time we arrived at our destination the two of us looked like we'd been to war. The windows had been wide open because it was so scorching hot and our sweaty faces had attracted the dust thrown into the air by the travelling car, so that we looked as if we were absolutely filthy. I glanced over at Dawn and her dark hair was standing up on end, her eye makeup that she had reapplied so carefully on the plane before disembarking was streaked across her face so she looked like Alice Cooper in one of his more aggressive videos. Sweat patches stood out on her tight-fitting khaki outfit. I hoped I looked better. "How do I look?" I asked her.

She burst out laughing. "No one has ever looked worse."

The only thing that kept us sane on the journey was the captivating landscape and incredible scenery. It became easy to forget about the heat as we passed through the most glorious countryside... we watched baboons playing in the trees and birds dancing in sunny skies. When we arrived at Sanbona, the tensions of the flight and the heat of the journey melted into calmness and serenity. The beauty of the place was breathtaking.

The driver told us on the journey down that it hadn't rained for weeks so the animal and plant life were struggling. The difference between rain and no rain in the UK may amount to little more than the difference between taking an umbrella and leaving it behind. Here it was a serious business, a matter of life and death. When there was no rain, the plants died so the herbivores couldn't eat, they grew weak and became easy prey so the predators thrived. The very balance of nature shifted a little on its axis with a turn in the weather.

As we drove past the guards and into the game reserve, we could see baboons all over the rocks. As we drove past, some of them started screaming.

"Why are they doing that?" asked Dawn.

"They have seen the lions coming, they are warning the other animals," said our driver.

"How clever," I said. "All the animals looking out for one another."

"To a degree," said the driver. "Not always. Now, keep your eyes peeled. If we are really lucky, you will see the lions."

It didn't strike me as all that lucky to see lions, but I knew what he meant...seeing any of the magnificent big creatures that we only ever read about in books would be amazing. To see one on our first day would be great.

Sanbona was set in a beautiful 130,000-acre wildlife reserve at the foot of the Warmwaterberg Mountains in the Karoo region, an area rich with vast plains, rivers, lakes and a huge array of animals.

My heart was pounding a little in my chest at the thought of the days ahead and everything we might see. I looked over at Dawn and she grabbed my hand and gave it a small squeeze. "I'm so excited," she said.

"Me too. Thank you for inviting me," I said.

"That's okay I couldn't have invited anyone else," she said.

I had no idea what that meant, but I was just thrilled to be there and thrilled that I was the only person she thought she could invite. It was kind of sweet.

That night we went to our rooms to unpack, we had separate rooms with a shared bathroom linking them. Dinner was to be in the outdoor restaurant, looking out into the magnificent countryside. We would be met by Henrique, the manager of the reserve, who would run through how things would work.

Henrique was a tall, slim, gangly man who looked like he'd never had a decent meal in his life. The polar opposite, in fact, of Dawn and me. He greeted us warmly and told us about the days ahead. There would be very early starts, and that way we would see lots of animals. Our ranger would meet us at breakfast at 4am to tell us about the route we would be taking. I glanced at Dawn. We were both thinking about Pieter...wonderful, fantastic Pieter who we were about to meet.

"There will be four other people in your group...a newly married couple called David and Alexa and two men: Patrick and Chris."

Dawn looked at me; I looked at Dawn. One handsome ranger and two unaccompanied men. Let the party start.

We sat there, enjoying pre-dinner drinks, and looking out into the starry sky. It felt like we were the only people on earth. It was all so beautiful, so serene. Then we saw flashes of lightning ahead of us, growing brighter and more intense as the evening wore on. By the time we had dinner, the wildest light show played out in the darkness, then thunder's heavy drum beat joined the cacophony, and the rain came...a little at first, then tumbling down to the delight of everyone.

"It's rain!" screamed the head chef, running outside and praying up to heaven. "Thank God. It's rain."

CHAPTER FOUR

"Dawn, Dawn," I said.

Silence.

"Dawn?"

Still nothing.

Oh God. This holiday might have been the biggest mistake of my entire life.

"Dawn," I tried again, louder this time. Still nothing.

It turned out Dawn snored. When I say 'snored' I mean she made such a bloody racket that she could have woken the dead. It was a sort of loud honking that left the room reverberating to its tune. I was surprised the whole place didn't wake up. I'd been standing in the bathroom shouting to her...it was no good...I walked through to her room and saw her lying sprawled across the bed – a hefty woman in a pair of men's pyjamas, wearing an eye mask that she'd clearly nicked from the plane.

"Dawn?"

It was no good...I couldn't rouse her at all. At least it didn't seem quite as loud now. When I'd been lying in bed it had been unbearable. I walked back into my room, opened the doors and strode out onto the balcony. Once I opened the patio doors, though, the noise became even louder. Good God alive – what on earth was going on with that woman...her snoring was so catastrophic that it somehow bounced through the walls and appeared to be coming from the lake outside. What sort of woman made that level of noise? I looked out over the water, shaking my head in disbelief, and that's when I spotted them; hippos...a whole load of them...honking wildly.

Ahhh...it wasn't Dawn at all. I smiled to myself. It might be judicious to keep to myself the fact that I'd confused her with a whole load of honking hippos. I scuttled back to bed, walking passed the gorgeous cream outfit I'd laid out for tomorrow. My size 20, elastic waist trousers in a soft cream colour, a white chiffon blouse, white long, flowy jacket and a straw bonnet that I had tied a cream ribbon round. Next to them sat my enormous knickers and heavily constructed support bra. I was really excited about striding out in my finery tomorrow. I knew it was a bit over the top, but I was sure the others would be dressed up – it wasn't every day you went on a bloody safari, was it?

Morning arrived with all the subtlety of a nuclear explosion. It turned out that Dawn had the world's loudest and most annoying alarm clock. Really, it was absolutely terrible; it made the honking hippos from last night sound like choirboys. I took my eye shield off, sat up and look into the darkness.

"We've got to get up," I shouted through to Dawn. "It's 3:45am."

This was the sort of time I should be coming in from a wild night of dancing and drinking, not getting up. But this was the thing with safaris, it was all about early mornings if you wanted to catch the animals before the day got hot and they disappeared from view – into the undergrowth away from the hot African sun.

There was no sound from Dawn. "Hello, are you awake?" I asked.

As I prepared to get up and go and find her, the bathroom door swung open and Dawn walked out.

"Oh," I said. "You're up already?" Then, "OH!" when she put on the light and I saw her in all her glory. She was dressed all in cream...like Meryl Streep from Out of Africa. Exactly as I'd been planning to dress. She even had cream crocheted gloves and a ribbon trailing from the hat perched on her newly styled hair.

"What the hell are you wearing?" I asked.

"You can see what I'm wearing," she replied. She was wearing tonnes of makeup as well.

"What I can see is that you're wearing the same thing that I was going to wear. Exactly the same clothes as I'd planned to."

"Well, not exactly the same," she said, indicating the cream shawl and the fact that she was wearing a long white skirt and not trousers.

"OK, not exactly but - you know - you've copied my look.

"How can I have copied it if I was dressed first?"

"Oh God, forget it," I said, clambering out of bed and heading for the bathroom. I did my make up as carefully as possible, determined to look better than her. At least I was thinner, and there weren't too many people I could say that about.

We descended the stairs and I knew how ridiculous we must look; two heavily overweight ladies with piles of makeup on, draped in ridiculous amounts of cream lace and white cotton. I was cross that we both had the same hat - bonnets bedecked with ribbons. Down below us, the others in our group looked askance. They were in fleeces, woolly hats and jeans.

Everyone was staring at us. I mean everyone...just staring: open-mouthed in disbelief at these two heavily overweight women who looked like they'd stepped out of a coffee plantation from the 1920s.

"Hello ladies," said the hotel manageress, breaking the silence. Her name was Carmella...we'd seen her briefly when Henrique had introduced her last night.

"How lovely to meet you properly. You both look so – well – amazing. Gosh.. I am so looking forward to seeing your blog. It's very exciting to have two famous British bloggers with us," she said.

"I'm the blogger, Mary is my friend," said Dawn, territorially. I had no desire to take any damn credit for her blog.

"But didn't we agree that the blog from the safari would be called 'Two Fat Ladies'?" said Carmella.

"Um, yes," said Dawn.

"Two Fat ladies?" I said.

"Yep," said Dawn.

"Really? Is that why you want me to come? Because I'm fat?"

"Well, kind of," she replied. "I needed someone fat to come with me to get the gig. And also you're fun too. I always liked you at school."

"Bloody hell, Dawn," I said. I don't know why I was offended. It's not like I could insist that I wasn't fat, it just seemed a bit - well - cruel - not to tell me why she'd invited me.

"Do join us for a cup of tea before we head out to meet your ranger," said Carmella, papering over the awkwardness. "Let me introduce you to the group."

There were two couples coming with us on the trip: David and Alexa who were on their honeymoon and seemed just to want to be alone, understandably. Alexa was a very beautiful and very young girl, David was much older...a good 20 years older to be honest. And he seemed wildly possessive of his young bride. I tried to talk to her twice and he all but shooed me away from her, wrapping his arms around her and claiming her as his own.

"He's bloody nuts," said Dawn. She was talking to me much more now, presumably spurred into social interaction by her embarrassment at getting caught out with the blog name.

"What possible danger does he think Alexa will come to just by talking to us?"

"God knows!" I replied. "It's not as if she's that interesting in any case. I'm quite happy not to talk to her; I was only being polite."

As well as David and Alexa there were the two men that we'd been told about: Patrick and Chris. They seemed really nice, and I had high hopes of friendships, and maybe even something more if they played their cards right.

Chris was an artist of some sort - he said he did modern, progressive art, and his most recent works were shortlisted for the Turner prize, which even I know is a big deal. He was great fun. Patrick was a food writer who did columns for men's magazines about restaurants and recipes.

While Chris was quite gnome-like, with a full-beard and sparkly, mischievous eyes and there was nothing particularly handsome about him; Patrick was gorgeous...classically beautiful with a square jaw and deep set, dark, brooding eyes.

The thing was though, even though Patrick was 50 million times more handsome, I found myself much more drawn to Chris - he had such a fabulous personality that he seemed good looking. Attractive personalities can make people seem so much more beautiful, can't they? Infact, there's nothing more attractive than a lovely personality...kindness and funny always beat square jaws and muscular torsos. Well, usually. I suppose it depends how muscular.

Sebastian smiled at me and offered an Elvis Presley-type sneer as he shook my hand; Chris wrapped me in a big hug. That was the difference between them.

The other difference was that Chris was wildly politically incorrect and seemed to constantly embarrass Patrick.

"Does anyone want to ask anything before we go out?" Carmella asked.

"Any lesbian animals?" asked Chris, with a glint in his eye.

We watched as Carmella raised her eyebrows and racked her brain trying to remember anything she might have learned about animal lesbianism at ranger school.

"I think it might be time to head out now," she said, her cheeks scorched red and the question lying unanswered in the air.

CHAPTER FIVE

"OK," said Carmella. "Your guide will be here soon and we'll be going out. I'd just like to tell you a little bit about Sanbona. You'll find this a fascinating holiday...in many ways, all safari holidays are exactly the same in structure: you get up early and go out to spot as many animals as possible before coming back to relax awhile, then go out to look for more in the late afternoon. After that you enjoy sundowners and a magnificent sunset before a lavish dinner."

"Ooooo," said the assembled guests.

"But here's the rub," she continued. "The reality is that every safari you go on is completely different. Every time you go out you see something new and hear something you haven't heard before – honking hippos, roaring lions or singing birds. You are moved in a different way with every trip. Safaris are living, breathing holidays that create their own drama as they unfold. They're an unwritten script, an unfinished symphony – a blank page on which your own individual story unfolds every day. Every time you head out you have no idea what awaits you. That's why they're so magical and unique."

The lady had such a lovely, lyrical way of talking, it was a joy to listen to her and I found myself lost in her words. Even Chris had shut up and stopped with the stupid questions.

"Now, the important job of the day, I need to find out what you want for sundowners. Mary – what do you fancy?"

Damn, why did I have to go first? I find it hard enough to think of what drink I want when I'm standing at the bar and about to drink it. The idea of deciding now what drink I might want at 6pm tonight was very tough to come to terms with. "A white wine," I said, and Carmella made a note in a pad adorned with giraffes.

"No, no. I'll have a Bailey's. Do you have Baileys?"

"We do," said Carmella, crossing out wine, and turning to the others to take their orders.

"No, I will have wine. Red wine though. That's what I fancy - a red wine."

"Right," she said, beginning to look as if she was losing patience with me. She crossed out Baileys with real vigour, and wrote in my latest fancy.

"OK, next," she said, and straight away, I knew that what I really wanted was a gin and tonic. I hovered on the edge of the group until she had done everyone but Dawn, then raised my hand like a schoolgirl.

"Sorry, but can I have gin and tonic instead? I promise I won't change my mind again."

"OK," she said, grimacing.

"I'll have a vodka and Red Bull," said Dawn.

"Ooooo..." I said, but Carmella was having none of it. The notebook had been put away and she was gathering up her things.

"Now then, let's go outside and introduce you to the ranger who'll be looking after you during your stay."

This was the moment that Dawn and I had been looking forward to since first seeing Pieter's heavenly smile on the website. We both adjusted our outfits and straightened our bonnets. I hoped the fact that we looked like extras from a Jane Austen serialisation wasn't going to put him off.

"Do go outside and we'll get going," she said, ushering us towards the door where an attractive, dark haired woman was standing.

"This is Cristine, she will be your guide while you are staying with us at Sanbona."

"What?" Dawn and I looked at one another in amazement. A WOMAN. This was not right at all.

"It's lovely to meet you all," said Cristine. "I'll be looking after you during your stay. As long as you do what I say, I will be able to show you all the amazing animals we have here at Sanbona and I'll be able to protect you and keep you safe. Please remember that this is not a zoo; these animals are wild. It's important to treat them with respect and to follow the basic rules that I will outline to you as we go round. The first rule is always to stay on the Land Rover, don't get off for any reason. If you drop something; tell me – don't try to get out to retrieve it. Understood?"

There were muted sounds of agreement from us all but I was too alarmed to join in.

"Any questions?" she asked, but the only question I had was WHERE THE HELL IS Pieter?

We left the luxury of the lodge and were immediately confronted by a muddy and filthy-looking vehicle. I realised in that second that I could not have been more inappropriately dressed. The Land Rover seemed to be terrifyingly open to the elements and rather too exposed considering I was dressed like a bridesmaid and we were going off to see animals that could tear us apart with their teeth.

I stood near the side, waiting for them to lower the steps for me to climb in.

"Just hop on board," said Cristine. Everyone clambered onto the vehicle except for Dawn and me. I knew there was no way on earth that I could get on there.

"Up you get," said Cristine.

"I'm not sure I can," I said.

I gave it a go, grabbing the handrail and trying to lumber myself on, but I just couldn't manage it.

"Hang on," said Cristine, running round to assist me. She stood behind and pushed on my bottom, trying to heave me on board. Embarrassingly it wasn't enough.. Dawn joined in and the two of them pushed with all their might as if trying to load an old sofa into a skip. Finally I was in - head first, and with all my dignity gone, but I was in. Next it was time to get Dawn on board. Carmella was called, then a guy sweeping the pathways came running and the chef who'd been dancing in the rain the night before...together they huffed and puffed and loaded Dawn on board.

"OK, lovely, no problem," said Dawn, doing her best to hide the embarrassment we we both suffering. As we were about to set off, Henrique came running along with a step ladder. "Just to make things a bit easier," he said. Cristine stored it in the back and we were finally ready to hit the road.

"Everyone comfortable?" she asked, when she'd returned to her seat.

"Are there lots of rangers?" I asked, completely ignoring her question about our comfort. Of course I wasn't comfortable, I was squeezed into a ropey old four by four next to a huge woman with thighs the size of fridges. My elegant bonnet was precariously placed and my clothes were dishevelled and certainly weren't comfortable. Even the elasticated trousers felt like they were digging into me which is against all the rules of elasticated clothing; their very existence depends on them being comfortable.

"There are 12 rangers here at Sanbona," she replied.

"All men?" I ventured.

"Yes, I'm the only women. Though around Africa there are increasing numbers of female rangers. You'll find that..."

"Do you know a ranger called Pieter?" I asked, cutting through her speech about female emancipation.

"Yes, he's the head ranger," said Cristine.

"Will we get to see him?"

"Sure you will," she said. "Is there any particular reason? If there's anything you need or want you can just ask me. I can help."

"No, that's fine. Just checking then. Um, so, when are we likely to meet Pieter? Do you know?"

"Will we see lots of animals?" asked Alexa.

"It's impossible to know," said Cristine."The thing with safaris is..."

"Right," I interrupted. "Just so we're clear – is it impossible to know whether we'll see Pieter, or not sure whether we'll see animals?"

"Animals!" said Cristine, quite sharply. I could tell she was getting fed up with me. To be honest, I think she was fed up with me the minute she saw me. Cristine was thin and wiry and dressed in khaki shorts and shirt. She was a no nonsense, outdoorsy sort of woman and I don't think she'd ever in her life before seen anyone as fat as me. Or as oddly dressed. Or as utterly useless at getting into a Land Rover.

"OK," I replied, sitting back in my seat.

"Good try," said Dawn, expressing a sliver of solidarity.

I'd positioned myself so I was near to Chris and Sebastian...they were on the seats just in front of us. It meant the lion would get to them first, which was reassuring. It also meant that I could talk to him as we bumbled along down the bumpy roads. I might have to turn my attentions to one of them if Pieter wasn't going to make an appearance. That's when I noticed they were holding hands.

Fuck! Two thirds of the single men were gay and the other third hadn't made an appearance. This wasn't going at all well.

CHAPTER SIX

"Now the thing with a safari," said Cristine. "Is that you never know what you're going to see, or not going to see."

"Too bloody right," I whispered to Dawn. "You head out expecting to see a gorgeous ranger with big thighs and a deep voice and end up with a woman."

"Don't make the mistake of thinking that this is like going to the theatre or something," Cristine was continuing. "The animals don't come out and perform for you. To be honest – we might see nothing at all today."

"We saw nothing yesterday," said Chris. "No bloody animal in sight yesterday." His voice rose theatrically as he spoke, and he stroked his beard, like some great Hollywood actor. Kind of like Brian Blessed might look if he lost about 10 stone.

"We saw birds, but they don't really count, do they?" said Patrick, shaking his head as if the lack of animals was entirely Cristine's fault.

"Well, hopefully we'll see something today," she replied. I had no idea how she kept her cool, really. She must have seen all manner of strange people gathering on the back of her landrover over the years, but we seemed like a particularly motley crew. I vowed to be as nice to her as possible for the remainder of our trip.

"So, we'll head off now," she said, pulling away from the safety of the lodge and driving through the huge fences into animal land. "No one must get out of the vehicle under any circumstances. As long as you stay inside, I can protect you. I have a gun here and I've worked here for a long time. I know what to do, but you must not get out of the Land Rover whatever happens. Do you all understand?"

We nodded mutely.

What animals are you hoping to see?"

There were mumblings about cheetahs and lions, and Dawn rather alarmingly growled that she'd love to see a kill: "I'd like to see a lion tear down an animal twice its size and drag it off while it's still alive," she said.

"Blimey - I'd just love to see some giraffes and elephants," I said plaintively. I've always thought that giraffes were sublimely elegant creatures - their gentle movements and that elegant long neck...kind of what I'd love to come back as if I had the choice. Elephants are great too, with their long trunks and comical flappy ears, and baby elephants are adorable.

"OK, I'll do my best," said Cristine.

Within minutes, as if ushered onto stage by an almighty director, giraffes moved ahead of us, gliding with such gracefulness through the trees, that tears sprang into my eyes. They had lovely long necks and tiny heads...the supermodels of the animal world.

Without being able to help it, I squealed a little. This was amazing. I mean AMAZING. If you've never been on a safari - go on one. They are bloody fantastic. I mean fantastic. To be fair, I only came for a free holiday, and to oggle the handsome rangers, I didn't think about how properly captivating it would all be.

Next came the elephants.

"You're good!" I told Cristine, as a herd of elephants trooped past us. The two animals I most wanted to see had appeared one after the other.

They lumbered close to the vehicle, and Cristine seemed quite comfortable. I was expecting her to drive away but she didn't move. I was so pleased. I wanted to stay here forever, close to these majestic, beautiful creatures. "No sudden movements and no sudden noises," she dictated. "But, besides that - don't worry -

elephants are gentle creatures. They express all sorts of emotions. Elephants cry when other elephants die...you see tears in their eyes when they are sad. They are very lovely. So intelligent, kind, sensitive and emotional, as long as you don't do anything to frighten them they will be quite comfortable in your company."

It turned out that Cristine was a world expert on elephants (how cool is that? Fancy being a global expert in elephants – that's the coolest thing in the world). She explained that she was studying their behaviour for a master's degree.

"Oh, hang on." With that, she jumped out of the driving seat and excitedly collected their droppings, displaying them for us to see. "Look," she said, as if showing us a diamond ring. "Aren't they lovely?" The droppings carry information about what the elephants have been eating that is useful for her research.

"I'm a very happy girl now," she said, dropping the contents of her gloved hand into a metal dish. "Lovely to have some fresh dung to play with tonight."

We saw so many animals that morning, it's hard to recount them all...a young tawny male lion trying to bring down an eland, failing miserably and having to wander away with his tail between his legs. Then another lion had been spotted by a fellow ranger, so we were invited to go along and take a look. This was a white lion – a beautiful beast - white of fur and with the pale blue-green eyes of a film star. When we reached him he was stretched out in the sun, his handsome face framed with great mane of white fluff, his protruding belly testament to a good feed. A couple of feet away from him, under the trees, out of the sun, lay the remains of a baby giraffe that he had killed that morning. "Can we get closer?" said Dawn, practically hanging out of the Land Rover to get a better look. "Can we go down there and take a look?"

"Really?" asked Cristine, losing her relaxed aura for a minute and giving Dawn a confused grin. "You want to go and stand between a male lion and his kill?"

"But he's lying down, he's full up, he's not going to be bothered by me. If he was, he'd have come up here and attacked the vehicle.

"It doesn't work like that," said Cristine. "Lions completely ignore safari vehicles. They're just large, unthreatening, moving things that don't look very appetising and smell strange. If you get out you instantly look like a meal – with a head and legs and a tasty aroma of meat."

"OK," said Dawn, suitably chastised. "But if it's a slower animal that we could outrun, can we get out and go up to see them?"

"No," said Cristine. "The thing I want you to remember is that for these animals - food runs. If something runs away from them, they'll assume they can eat it. And don't be fooled into thinking you can out-run anything. It may look big and fat, but even a hippo can run as fast as Usain Bolt and swim faster than Michael Phelps, and a rhino can run over 30mph. You wanna take on one of those?? Not on my watch."

"What should we do if we're chased by a hippo then?" asked Dawn.

"Well, hopefully you won't be, but if you are, I'd suggest climbing a tree."

We all nodded to ourselves, thinking this wise advice, and words that we would definitely be heeding should rhinos or hippos get in our paths.

We were only out for a few hours in the morning and Cristine told us it was one of the best mornings of sightings she'd ever seen. I tried to persuade her that the animals had come to see Dawn and me in our finery...I even doffed my ribbon bedecked straw hat in her direction, but she wasn't having any of it.

"It's because of the rain last night," she concluded. "It has brought them all out for the first time in ages.

In the late afternoon we went back out and saw rhinos and buffalos aplenty. I learned all about the safari world...how the buffalos die off first if there is a drought because they need so much water.

We saw birds and plants as well. My God, the birds were spectacular – from secretary birds which take off like aeroplanes, with a giant run up, spreading their wings and swooping into the sky; to the huge fish eagles and the staggeringly pretty smaller birds in jewel-like colours, singing beautifully through the warmth and silence in this lovely part of the world. By the end of it, I was hopelessly in love with Cristine and wanted to stay here forever, learning from her and mixing with these fabulous animals.

CHAPTER SEVEN

It was 6pm, a very special time of day...sundowner time. This, in case you were unaccustomed to the ways and mores of the Safari set, was shorthand for drinking! It took place when the sun was just going down so the ranger headed for the most picturesque spot imaginable, and we all consumed the drinks that we'd selected that morning. Cristine had chosen the place with the best view of the sunset and we were all set to enjoy assorted snacks and large drinks in front of the magnificent view.

We pulled up at the breathtakingly pretty spot and Cristine began unloading the goodies she had packed into her cool bag. There was an alarming moment when it occurred to me that the pots containing crisps and nuts were astonishingly similar in appearance to the pots she had used earlier to capture elephant dung. I decided to share this with the group. It didn't go down well. We all steered clear of the chocolate peanuts after that.

Cristine handed me a gin and tonic and handed Dawn her vodka and redbull. As soon as I saw her drink I immediately wished I had ordered one as well. My gin and tonic seemed far less exciting in both colour and flavour. I grimaced at Cristine like it was her fault, but she seemed oblivious to my facial expressions, so I took a huge gulp and felt the warming drink move down my throat like an anesthetic and into my stomach where it warmed me from within.

"Cheers," said Sebastian, and we all raised our glasses. I released that I was the only one to have taken a huge gulp before the 'cheers–ing' has been done.

"Cheers," I joined in, raising my glass with everyone else. We all sipped our drinks while zebras moved easily across the plane in front of us.

"See how the baby zebras stay close to their mums," said Cristine. "That's so that the calf is camouflaged by the mum's stripes. Look...you can't see the baby next to mum...the stripes blend into one another."

We looked over and I could see what she meant. Nature was so clever.

"Wouldn't the lion just attack the mum anyway?" asked Dawn.

"Could do...but mums are harder to attack than babies, and babies taste better. Younger meat."

"Down in one," said Chris, slightly ruining the rarified atmosphere. "Come on - 1,2,3 and we all down our drinks."

"Excellent. Is there any other way?" I said, throwing my gin and tonic down my throat and smiling broadly. Chris downed his too. The others just looked at us while they sipped theirs.

"We're not 14," said Alexa, which felt slightly ironic since she was the only one in the group who looked as if she might actually be 14.

"It's a holiday," I said, exasperation dancing through my voice. "Chill out."

The only problem with downing your drink was that it was then all gone. Chris and I looked at one another, as the others continued to sip. Then there was a quite magical moment. A second of pure joy. Cristine unzipped her cool bag and revealed that she had more drink in there.

"Another G&T?" she asked. "And a red wine for you, Chris?"

Honestly, I could have kissed her.We both nodded vigorously and laughed as we caught each other's eyes. Suddenly it felt like Chris and I would end up the best of friends after all this.

"Cheers!"

We both downed our drinks again. The others had wandered off to the other side of the small area we'd stopped in. It was a lovely little place...a little grassy area with a couple of trees, three benches facing out towards the most beautiful views and a big, wooden table. Buried deep in the undergrowth in front of the area was an old shack that we could just about make out, it was surrounded by trees and apparently contained an ancient toilet. I decided to hang on until we were back in the room before going to the loo. I didn't fancy wandering down there, through the undergrowth.

Though the others wandered around to look at the views from all sides, and compare notes on the incredible day we'd just had, Chris and I stayed close to Cristine and her cool bag. Our devotion to her paid off when she unzipped the bag and took out more drinks. Jesus, how big was that bag? It seemed to have endless amount of drink in it. I vowed to ask her where she got it from and buy myself one.

"I only brought three of everyone's drinks," she said, as she pulled out gin and wine. I didn't think people would want more than that, since this is just a quick stop off to see the sunset and not a massive piss-up or anything."

Alright, alright, I thought. Cut it with all the judgement.

"Perhaps we should drink these more slowly," said Chris.

Cristine looked out at the others, chatting happily in the distance.

"Unless the others don't want theirs, of course," she said. "Then you could have more."

"They definitely won't want theirs," Chris and I said at exactly the same time.

The thing was, I didn't imagine that the others did want their drinks...they were too busy chatting and admiring the views.

"I'll go for a vodka and redbull," I said.

"Yeah, I'll have Patrick's red wine," said Chris and we downed them both while Cristine looked on, eyebrows raised and hand poised on the cool bag so she could replenish us when necessary, looking increasingly alarmed at the speed of our drinking, despite her professional demeanour.

"What's next?" asked Chris.

"What did the Americans order?" I asked.

I felt quite drunk now. It felt lovely, to be honest. That lovely light-headed feeling you get before the real feeling of hopeless drunkenness hits.

"Just these dwarf bottles of vodka and coke," said Cristine, pulling them out of the cool bag,

"Dwarf!" said Chris, convulsing into laughter. "Dwarf. That's so funny."

"Yes, funny word," I said, though I didn't think it was funny at all, really. Perhaps Chris was way drunker than me?

"No - not the word. It's just the...ah, it's hard to explain."

"Try," I said.

"OK, well I need to tell you about our parties."

"Good, then tell me," I said, indicating to Cristine that we'd like the bottles of vodka and coke despite Chris's hysterics.

"Well," he said, smiling to himself. "We really like to party... Or, should I say, I like to party, and Patrick just tolerates it."

"Go on..." I said, taking a big sip of my drink.

"We have these parties and they're full of great people. You know, writers, artists, musicians... Just brilliant people who are so talented and artistic, and I want to make sure they have the best time possible, so the food I prepare is always magnificent – I will get someone in to make sure the food is restaurant quality, and I serve the best wines and champagne, and then – when everyone is drunk and having a great time and I'm thinking things just can't get better...that's when the dwarves come."

"Dwarves?"

"Yep. Tons of dwarfs. Dwarves everywhere."

"I'm really confused, you have to tell me what the dwarves are there for."

"So people can snort cocaine off their heads. Why else would they be there?" he said.

I just looked at him, eyebrows raised, mouth open.

"Have you never done that?" he said, looking genuinely surprised.

"No, of course I fucking haven't. What's wrong with you?"

He laughed like a drain. "Gosh, you are funny. You have to try it. Snorting cocaine off the head of a dwarf is the best fun you can ever have. You are coming to the next party, just don't bring that bloody friend of yours; she is no fun."

"Okay, I will come," I said tentatively.

"Brilliant," he said. "You won't have to bring anything. I will supply the food, and the booze. Oh, and the dwarves."

It wasn't long before the effects of the alcohol really kicked in and I found myself staggering, swaying, slurring and unbearably desperate for the loo. I was aware that going for a wee here necessitated me striding through the undergrowth in the direction of the small wooden shack. Before I'd been quite worried about it, but with the false confidence granted by alcohol, it didn't seem to be half the problem.

"I'm going to have to go to the loo," I said to Cristine, shuffling a little as I lost my balance.

"Of course. It's all open - so just go inside, but remember to shut the door afterwards so snakes don't go in there.

"Snakes?" I gasped.

"You're on safari," she said. "There are snakes everywhere."

Chris did a sort of little jumpy skip on the spot at the thought of them; it made me like him even more.

"I'm not a fan of snakes," he said. I could see on his face that was a great understatement. He looked bloody terrified. To be honest, who is a fan of snakes? Only spotty teenagers with personality disorders who keep them in their bedrooms and feed them live rats.

"It'll be fine," said Cristine, she looked rather amused by it all.

" Will you come down with me?" I asked her, feeling like a lemon, but now worried at what I might find down there.

"Okay," she said, leading the way towards the shack, a gun in her hand.

"What on earth do you need the gun for?" I asked.

"To shoot the snakes," she said.

"You are joking!" I squealed, terror resonating through my voice.

"Yes I am, hah!" She said. "I've just got my gun with me because we're not supposed to leave them lying around. I didn't fancy leaving it next to a drunk Chris. I'd come back and find he'd shot himself in the foot or something."

"Yes, very wise," I replied. Cristine was quite funny really, once again I felt quite sorry for her having to deal with drunk English people when I'm sure she'd much rather have been studying elephants and talking to people who understood these things far better than we ever would.

She led the way through the undergrowth, knocking it aside as she went, purposefully striding with all the confidence of a woman who does this every day. I stayed close behind, jumping and screaming as every blade of grass touched me, now paranoid that there were snakes everywhere.

"Here we are then," said Cristine, opening the door to the wooden shack, leaning inside putting on the antiquated light. It was a very basic, very outdoorsy sort of toilet, but it was clean, there was a sink and there was – crucially – toilet paper. To be honest, it was all you could ever reasonably expect from a toilet in the middle of the wilds of Africa.

I walked inside, dropped my cream trousers and crouched down gently. When anything is old looking I'm always extra cautious because I know I'm a huge weight and likely to break things. Breaking the toilet into would be too embarrassing for words, so I hovered slightly above it. That's when I saw it...in the corner of the room – a snake.

It's difficult to describe the huge scream that came from my mouth – driven by some inner terror and fear. I'd never made a noise quite like it before. I heard rustling outside as someone came down the hill to my aid. I knew I should pull up my trousers and make myself decent, but I was so paralysed by fear, so utterly terrified, I couldn't move. The wooden door opened and Chris's face peered through, seeing me sitting there with my lovely, frilly knickers around my ankles.

"I'm terrified," I said to Chris. "It's over there..."

I pointed to the corner of the room where the green snake lay.

I kept my voice low, eager not to disturb the vile creature in anyway.

"Oh my fucking God!" screamed Chris at the top of his voice, piling back out through the door and running with all his might. At the top of the hill, Cristine had wandered back to the Land Rover and had started packing away the snacks.

I was alone

The only positive thing in this terrible scenario was that Chris's enormous scream didn't seem to have disturbed the snake in any way, and it sat there not moving, coiled, poised, and ready to strike if my guard should be let down at any stage.

I knew I had to stand up from this uncompromising position, and get myself out of the room, but I was terrified to move.

Slowly I grabbed my trousers and knickers and tiptoed towards the door. I pulled the big wooden door towards me and it made a horrible squeaking sound. Oh God, that was bound to alert the creature. I threw myself out into the undergrowth, convinced the snake was following me but too scared to look behind. All I could think of was Cristine's advice to climb a tree. There was a big tree with low branches just to the left of me. I kicked off my trousers that were round my ankles, and grabbed at my knickers, half pulling them up. From the corner of my eye I could see that the party of fellow Safari goers was starting to move down the hill. Chris was in the middle, pointing towards me, presumably telling them the story about the snake in the corner of the toilet.

I launched myself up into the arms of the tree, sure that if I was off the ground, my chances of being attacked by the horrible bright green slippery reptile were vastly reduced. I sat on the branch and looked down, Cristine was walking towards me, she would save me. She had a gun and she was used to this sort of thing. I was bound to be safe.

"Are you okay?" she asked. I'd lost the power of speech, my fear having robbed me of any ability to articulate the sheer terror coursing through my veins.

I reached up to the branch just above, planning to climb onto it, but unsure whether it was wise. I was drunk, trouserless and terrified; was tree climbing the best idea right now? I just felt as if I would be safer the higher I got off the ground.

"Stay there, Mary," said Cristine. "Don't move okay, I don't want you to fall."

I clung on for dear life as Cristine reached for her radio, and called for help, asking for another ranger to come and assist her.

I really wished I hadn't climbed up the tree. Every time I looked down I felt sick, every time I looked out across the landscape I became convinced that snakes were coming from everywhere to get me, and down below I saw the fellow Safari-goers assembling. They shouted up words of comfort, and told me to hang on and everything would be okay. Cristine was going to get rid of the snake, she was just waiting for assistance to arrive, then she'd take care of everything.

"You okay?" she said. "I mean – you're not gonna fall are you?"

"No," I said, with more surety than I felt. I was half-pissed, there was every chance of me falling from the tree.

Over at the top of the hill Dawn was waiting, she hadn't come down to join the others and reassure me about my fate. Instead she was taking videos of me for her blog. It struck me that I was either going to be eaten alive by snakes, or be featured on a blog wearing my knickers and with my stomach hanging out. I wasn't entirely sure which was the worst of the two options. Perhaps both would happen! I was fairly confident that even if I were being eaten by snakes, Dawn would keep filming.

CHAPTER EIGHT

I heard the Land Rover bringing my rescuers before I saw it. It arrived at the top of the hill, pulling up by the picnic table where we'd been having such a lovely drink and chat just 15 minutes earlier. I could hear a handbrake being pulled on...then I saw him - like a superhero striding onto a movie set: Pieter. The magnificent, gorgeous, handsome Pieter, powering down the hill to save me. I just wished I looked better. This wasn't in any way how I'd hoped to appear when he first set eyes on me. I'd pictured myself like Meryl Streep, reclining decoratively in a wicker chair, sipping champagne; not half-pissed and clinging onto the trunk of a tree, terrified out of my mind, with my trousers on the ground in front of me.

"There's a green mamba in the toilets and a lady in the tree," said Cristine, her tone was quite matter of fact, as if this sort of thing happened every day. "Could you check on the snake first? I'll stay with tree lady."

Tree lady? Is this what I had been reduced to?

Pieter smiled at Cristine and looked up at me.

"You OK up there?" he asked.

"Yes, fine," I lied.

He strode manfully towards the toilets as Dawn appeared under the tree below me, still filming.

"He's hot," she said.

I should have realised that it was the arrival of the handsome ranger that had forced Dawn to come down the hill to join us, and not any concern for my well-being.

"Yep," I replied, noncommittally. Pieter certainly was drop dead gorgeous, but it was strange how much that didn't matter when you were stranded in a tree and just wanted someone kindly and non-judgemental to get you down. I guess I was scared, and when you're scared you want someone who cares by your side. I looked to Cristine for help, but she was watching Pieter's back as he went on a snake hunt. For the first time that holiday I really wished that Ted were there. Sensible, practical, reliable Ted would know exactly what to do...to be honest, he would probably have climbed up the tree by now and be helping me down, carefully and gently, telling me that none of this was my fault and that any one of us could have found ourselves stuck in a tree without trousers. It was to be understood. My tree climb was a sensible precaution, not the actions of a ridiculous, drunk woman.

"Was this the snake you were worried about?" said Pieter, walking towards the tree, holding the giant, luminous green snake in his hands.

"Oh my God, be careful," I said. "Those things are vicious."

I'd never seen anyone so brave in my life. How did he manage to carry it like that without looking utterly terrified? It was beyond me.

"I think I'll be okay," said Pieter with a slow smile. "This is a hosepipe."

"Oh!" I said. To say that I was embarrassed would be a dramatic understatement, I felt utterly ridiculous, crouching in the tree for no reason.

"Was this why are you ran up the tree?"

"Yes," I said. "I thought it was a snake... I just ran away and remembered Cristine's advice that it was best to run up a tree."

"From hippos," said Cristine. "Not snakes."

"Pretty weird place to hide from snakes," said Pieter. "Because - let's be honest, you get loads of snakes in trees, possibly more than you get on land."

"I didn't really think," I said, panicking a little at the thought. "I was scared."

"Do you want to get down now then?" he said.

"Yes, I really want to come down but I don't know how to," I said. I was aware that my words were vaguely slurring as I spoke. I wasn't full on drunk or anything, but things were swaying, and I knew there was no chance of me getting out of the tree unaided. Not without landing flat on my face and probably doing myself, and perhaps other people, serious injury.

Pieter was just looking at me.

"I still feel very shaky," I said. "I'm scared to come down."

"Okay then, I'll have to come up."

Pieter dropped the snake-like hose pipe onto the ground and climbed up to me with ease. He reached the branch on which I was perching in about a 10th of the time that it had taken me to get there. He crouched next to me. "How are we going to do this, then?" He asked, looking straight into my eyes.

He had these dreamy grey-green eyes that seemed to sparkle like a calm sea on a warm summer's day. He had been clean shaven in the images on the website, but today he had a rough looking beard which just seem to add to his beauty. He stroked his chin as he spoke, the glint in his eyes growing as he thought through the options for getting a very large lady out of a tree.

"How about if I climb down to the next branch, and help you down to it?" he said.

This didn't seem to be a very sophisticated plan, to be honest. But I knew I just had to do as I was told. "Okay, I'll try," I said.

"OK, move your right leg down towards this branch."

He was issuing instructions that were simple and straightforward and should have been easy to follow. Perhaps they would've been easy for someone more agile and less drunk. The trouble was that I couldn't lift my leg in the way he needed me to because my stomach was in the way. Only people who have been fat understand how debilitating it can be. I simply couldn't lift my leg up and over the branches to put it on the spot he recommended because my stomach was where he wanted my knee to go. Really he should have been able to see this, since it was all completely on show.

Eventually he realised the strategy was not going to work.

"Cristine, can you call for assistance please. Tell them to bring the winch."

"Oh my God, what are you going to do?" I said.

"I'm going to get you out of the tree," he said.

And so it was that on a cool April morning Mary Brown's mum casually switched on the computer in her suburban kitchen in the hope of catching a glimpse of her daughter enjoying the holiday of a lifetime. She was with three of the ladies from bridge club when Mrs Brown opened Dawn's blog to see her only daughter being winched out of a tree with her knickers fully on show, her hair sticking up everywhere, and a team of rangers attempting to move her as if she was a bull elephant that had got stuck in the mud.

"Goodness," said Margaret, Mrs Brown's long-standing bridge partner. "What a time she's having."

CHAPTER NINE

They got me down from the tree eventually, but I'd be lying if I said it was a simple procedure. By the time I was on the ground, my finger nails and dignity were completely trashed. I'd screamed the whole time which was very embarrassing – I just became convinced that I was going to fall and die. Infact, the only good thing to emerge from the whole, horrible tree incident, was that Pieter ended up promising me that he would take me to see the cheetah close up the next morning if I please just stopped screaming.

"Close up," I'd said through unattractive sobs.

"Close up," he confirmed. "We'll walk up to it so you can see it's beautiful coat. OK?"

"OK," I'd said. I realised he was talking to me as if I were a child but I didn't mind. I didn't mind anything at the time. I just wanted to be back in the room with my trousers on. That wasn't too much to ask, surely?

Pieter was true to his word and when we got back to the lodge he said he'd be back the next morning to pick me up. I went to bed feeling a little bit ashamed at the way the day had progressed, and a little chafed on my thighs where I'd been dragged out of the tree, but excited. I'd loved seeing all the animals, and the prospect of walking right up to the cheetah the next morning with Pieter was very appealing. It was also nice that I wouldn't have to get up at bloody 4am to do it. He assured me that if I let the others go off on their early morning drive, we'd leave later and go straight to where the cheetah always lay.

So, at 8am, I was sitting in the reception area, waiting for Pieter. Cheetahs were his favourite animal; he knew all about them – I don't think he was an academic like Cristine, he certainly didn't seem like someone who did much studying, but he certainly had lots of experience of working with them; he'd been around them a long time. I had a feeling that this was going to be the most amazing morning ever.

I heard the Land Rover pull up outside, and – just for extra measure – Pieter beeped loudly and shouted my name. I jumped up, grabbed my bag and ran outside. I felt like a girl going on a first date.

"Hello there," he said, waiting in the vehicle for me to climb in, clearly unaware what a problem it was for me to get into the damn thing. We'd resorted to using the step ladder yesterday and that had worked well, but Pieter didn't appear to be aware of the difficulties I'd had.

"I may need a hand," I said to Pieter, trying not to look too pathetic. "I'm not great at climbing into these things."

Of course, of course," he said, jumping down and running round to help me. Rather than give me a hand up he opted for pushing my bottom so that I went into the Land Rover headfirst again. This time I felt like a nervous foal been pushed onto the back of a horse truck against its wishes. Not the most unladylike or sophisticated moves by any definition, but at least I was in.

"If we get going, we'll catch up with the others by the rock on the far side where the cheetah tends to spend her time," said Pieter. The words stung like an arrow to the heart. "What do you mean? Meet up with the others?" I said. "I didn't realise they were coming."

"Yes, Cristine thought they might all enjoy it, so I said I would take them all. That's not a problem, is it?"

"No, no, not at all," I lied. It was a rubbish idea in so many ways...firstly because if we were catching up with the group, it meant I could have gone with them in the first place, and could have seen more wild animals. Also, it meant that Dawn would now be able to come and see the cheetah with us, and after the way she'd behaved yesterday... videoing me in my hour of great embarrassment, I didn't want her anywhere near me.

"Good – there they are now," he said, smiling and waving at Cristine. The two of them seemed to get on very well.

I'd had about 10 minutes alone with Pieter and we hadn't even had the chance to discuss cheetahs. The plan to spend time with him and learn everything I could collapsed beneath me.

Cristine jumped out of her Land Rover and grabbed her gun, the others all climbed out after her, waving to me. "Hey stranger, there you are. I was worried about you when you didn't turn up this morning. Are you OK?" said Chris.

"Hi, yes, I'm fine. Ego a bit bruised, but OK," I said.

"Listen, I wanted to apologise...I came to your room last night but the lights were off, and I didn't want to wake you up if you'd gone for an early night, but I did want to say sorry."

"What on earth for?" I asked.

"For being useless. For bursting into the loo and embarrassing you, then squealing and running out."

"Honestly, don't worry, I'd have done the same," I said, though I knew I wouldn't have. I knew I'd have tried to help.

On the far side of the Land Rover I saw Dawn grinning wildly. She waved over and lifted her video camera to her face. Honestly, I was ready to shove that thing down her throat.

Pieter ran through the way things would work. He would lead the way, and we were all to stay behind him and not run or move away from him whatever happened.

"I cannot protect you if you all run off in different directions," he said. "Just stay behind me and you will be safe. Understand?"

"Yes," we all chorused, it sounded amazing that he was going to lead us directly up to the cheetah. I shared my excitement with Dawn. But her face had turned a gentle shade of puce.

"He can't just walk up to a cheetah," she said. "That's insane."

"He knows what he's doing, don't worry," I said.

"Okay, everyone quiet," said Pieter ."Stay behind me in a line, Cristine will be at the back. We are both armed and you will be safe. But you must not run off or scream or make sudden movements... just follow and stay in a line directly behind me. Okay?"

"Can I just confirm? Are we going to walk directly up to the cheetah?" said Dawn. "I don't think that sounds very safe."

"You'll be safe as long as you stay behind me and do as I say," said Pieter, a hint of impatience creeping into his voice. I could understand why – he must have told us a dozen times that we'd be safe if we did as he said.

"Right, off we go then." Pieter walked forward, striding up towards the rock.

It was fascinating to be walking up to a wild animal. I felt completely safe with Pieter leading the way. I stayed right behind him, feeling the excitement grow as we walked, all of us in his footsteps as we headed towards the cat lounging in the sunshine slightly tucked into the shade, by the huge rock.

"Can you see," said Pieter, whispering as loudly as he dare so as not to alert the cat to our presence.

I could see the cheetah clearly; its gorgeous coat shimmering in the morning sun. Wow it was beautiful...I yearned to go closer still. As if sensing my thoughts, Pieter took a step towards the animal and we all followed suit. We were all silent, all that could be heard was the gentle sound of twigs snapping beneath our feet. Then, suddenly, there was a cry.

"Oh God I'm terrified," said Dawn. "It's gonna jump up and eat me, I just know it."

"Shhhhhh," said Pieter. "You have to keep quiet."

As he said this the cheetah opened its mouth to give a giant yawn and Dawn completely lost her mind. "Aaaahhhh," she screamed, dropping her video camera and rushing back towards the Land Rover, screaming at the top of her voice.

"For God's sake," Pieter said, turning sharply and indicating to Cristine to quieten the hysterical woman at all costs. I picked up her video camera which was still running and slung it over my shoulder.

I could see Dawn and Cristine fighting down by the Land Rover as Dawn continued to scream and declare that she knew the cheetah was going to eat us all.

"Aren't you going to video her?" Pieter said, winking at me. "This is the moment to get your revenge."

"That would be cruel," I said.

"She videoed you when you are stuck in a tree yesterday, And plastered it all over her blog," he said. "I was watching it last night – it was a nasty thing to do."

Oh no, Pieter had seen the video. I wondered who else had. I couldn't remember whether I'd given Ted the blog address...I really hoped not. Dawn was still shrieking.

"Go on, video her, you're missing it all," Pieter said.

I lifted the camera up and looked at it for a couple of seconds, then I turned it off.

"I don't want to behave like that," I said. "What she did to me was humiliating. I'd rather go through life without humiliating anyone"

"You are one hell of a woman, Mary Brown," said Pieter, turning to lead us back down towards the Land Rover. "That was a very kind thing to do."

"Thanks," I said, feeling myself turn red.

"Sorry we couldn't spend much time with the cheetah," he added. "I know you were very keen to see it, but it would have become terrified with all that screaming It wasn't safe to stay."

"I understand," I said. "I just really wanted to know more about them. Is it true that you're an expert. Kind of like a professor of cheetahs."

"Ha," he said. "I guess you could say that. I have lots of videos of the cheetah, right from when she was a cub, and pictures of her when she was pregnant and when she had her cubs. There are tonnes of research notes that the conservationists made and left copies of because they knew how much I loved her. I should bring them round some time for you to see?"

"Oh Pieter, I'd really love that," I said, gently touching his arm.

"OK, why don't you come over to mine tonight and we'll have a cheetah evening. How does that sound?"

"Oh thank you," that would be amazing," I said. "Thank you."

"No problem, I'll cook dinner or something," he said.

So, that was a surprise. It turned out that Pieter was a really nice guy despite being gorgeous enough to get away with being a shit. Who'd have thought?

CHAPTER TEN

The next day was really good fun out on safari, but we didn't see as many animals as the first day, and there was nothing special planned, like walking up to the cheetah or tracking the lions. We did go to see some rock art which was interesting, it was fascinating to think that so long ago people were turning to art to express themselves. It gave a real insight into their mindsets to see what they drew (men with spears, mainly! I guess they were pretty preoccupied with safety back then), but all I really wanted to do was drive around looking for animals. I loved seeing them. I even found myself feeling sad on the late afternoon drive that day when Cristine talked about going for sundowners.

I'd rather have had more time to look for rhinos or drive around in search of the elusive white lion.

Chris nudged me when I asked whether we could stay in the Land Rover instead of finding a place for drinks. "Don't spoil the fun...it's time for a drink," he chided. I smiled back, but the honest truth was that I'd much prefered to have looked for animals than drink gin and tonic...and that's something I never imagined myself saying.

Pieter was picking me up at 8pm that evening to take me to his house for our cheetah night so there wasn't too much time to prepare by the time we got back from animal watching and sundowners.

As soon as I got in, I tore off my clothes and lay back in a large spa bath, bubbles frothing all around me sending soft scents up into the air, as I lay back and breathed deeply. It was such a huge bath, it even covered me completely, which is a rarity. Most of the time in the bath I'm forever splashing water over me to keep myself covered. Infrequently I can't actually fit into the bath at all which is really bloody mortifying.

As I felt myself relax and melt into the soapy suds, my phone rang next to me.

"Hi gorgeous, how are you doing?"

It was Ted.

"You OK?" I asked.

"Yes, but missing you like mad," he replied. "It's lonely here without you. Are you missing me?"

"Of course I am," I replied. "I wish you were here instead of Dawn."

"Oh yes - so tell me - what's she like then? Is she good company?"

"She's OK," I replied. "I mean - she's let me come on a free holiday with her, so I can't complain too much, but she's quite - I don't know - she's not the friendliest person ever. I keep feeling like she's trying to make me look an idiot."

"You mean in the Two Fat Ladies blog?" he asked.

"Yes - exactly. She said we'd always got on at school and that's why she was inviting me on safari, but it turns out she only wanted me for the size of my arse...and there aren't many people saying that about me."

Ted laughed and told me not to worry.

"The blog's really funny," he said. "You up that tree was hysterical."

"Really?" I said. "Wasn't it mortifying? I haven't been able to bring to watch it...I imagined it was awful."

"Don't be silly," said Ted. "You looked scared, but you were still your usual funny self throughout."

"Thank you," I said, feeling a wave of warmth towards him.

"Who's Pieter?" asked Ted.

"Oh, no one. He's just one of the rangers here. Nothing special about him."

"He looks very handsome in the video."

"Ha!" I said. "Videos can be very deceptive indeed."

"Oh good," he said. "Because there's a whole montage of pictures on the site and it says you've got a hot date with him tonight."

"Whaaat? No – I haven't. It's not a date. For God's sake, Ted. Of course it's not a date. He's just going to talk to me about cheetahs."

"How appropriate," said Ted.

"Why's that appropriate? What are you talking about?"

"Well, you're going to be cheating on me. Seems appropriate."

"No, I'm not. This is insane. Ted, please don't make this into something it isn't. He's going to talk to me about cheetahs – the animals – like lions and leopards – I wanted to go and see the cheetah yesterday but Dawn got scared and screamed, so Pieter had to take us all away. He said he'd show me his collection of cheetah memorabilia tonight."

"His selection of cheetah memorabilia? Really? He couldn't do better than that?"

"He's a ranger, Ted. He's just trying to make sure I have the best possible experience while I'm here so we write nice things about him in the blog...that's all."

"OK," said Ted. "It's just hard, you know...reading all this stuff about you and seeing pictures of you having great fun with these gorgeous blokes, and I'm stuck at work."

"I would have stayed behind if you'd asked me to," I said. "You told me to go. You said you were really busy at work."

"I know," said Ted. "I know. I really wish I hadn't. I thought the break would do us good but I really miss you."

"It's only a couple more days," I responded. "And – you know – when you say 'having a great time with all these gorgeous men' – you're talking about me being stuck in a tree and having to be winched out. It wasn't the best time ever. It really wasn't. Whatever the guys may have looked like – it was bloody humiliating."

"No, I know. I'm sorry. Look you have a great time, OK?"

"I will," I reassured him. "And I'll see you in a few days."

"Look forward to it, angel," he said.

The call from Ted left me feeling a little shaken, as I clambered out of the bath, and dried myself on the softest, fluffiest towels known to man. I knew tonight wasn't a date that I was going on, but it was a shock how concerned Ted was. It was also a huge shock that he was reading the blog so closely. And why the hell was Dawn putting up all sorts of nonsense on there about me and Pieter? Why the hell would she do that?

I had been quite relaxed with her and uncritical while she'd exposed my imperfections and errors to the world but this just seemed a deliberate attempt to embarrass me.

I could see that a video of a fat woman in her knickers, stuck up a tree, was funny and would attract viewers and followers which, at the end of the day, was her job. I understood that. But putting a piece on there about me going on a date with Pieter...how was that supposed to do anything to drive traffic? She'd just got into the habit of putting everything on there, and simply wasn't stopping to think whether what she was doing could be perceived as being just a little cruel.

I sent a text to her. "Dawn, can you not put up stuff on the blog about me going on dates with Pieter. It's just a pleasant evening talking about cheetahs, not a date. My boyfriend saw the blog update and isn't very happy."

"Boyfriend?" replied Dawn. "I didn't know you had a boyfriend."

"You never asked," I replied.

"No, I suppose I didn't. I just assumed you didn't. I don't really think about people like us having boyfriends Well, behave yourself tonight then."

'People like us'? Thanks. By that I guess she meant 'fat people'. Charming.

Since the entire contents of the wardrobe I'd brought with me to South Africa comprised cream linen, white cotton and lace, I had no choice but to look like Meryl Streep's younger, fatter, uglier British cousin for my cheetah night, so, it was on with the lacy white top, and the long linen skirt. The straw hat was a bit much for evening wear, even I could see that, but I had a big cream jumper with me...kind of like a cricket jumper but without the cricket stripes on it...it would be perfect if the evening got cold. I draped it over my shoulders and pulled the lace top down. I needed the top to fall as low as possible to cover my horrible fat belly, but pulling it down meant that a whole load of cleavage was being shown. Given the choice between stomach and cleavage, I decided to go for the latter.

So, just for the record – my cleavage wasn't showing because I fancied Pieter or anything...my cleavage was showing in order to make sure my stomach was covered. Hope that's clear.

I wandered down the staircase to the reception area where I'd arranged to meet Pieter. It was a lovely old sweeping staircase that you'd imagine appearing in a Hollywood film. It was beautiful and I found myself throwing my hair back and striding confidently every time I walked down them.

"Oh, thank God," came a voice from down below. "Can someone help me?"

"Hello," I replied, walking towards the door from where the voice appeared to be coming. Just the other side of it stood Cristine, looking confused and holding out two sets of car keys.

"Can you drive, Mary?" she asked, looking at me appealingly.

"Sort of," I said. "I mean - I've had lessons but I never passed my test."

"That's OK. I don't need you to go on a public road, just to move this car forward while I move the Land Rovers in to get the oil checked. Pieter has offered to help me by bringing the barrells in."

"Yes," I said. "Which car though - I can't get into those Land Rovers, let alone drive them."

"This one," said Cristine, indicating a small car that I felt much more comfortable about trying to drive. It was around 100m away from where it needed to be. I could do that.

"Thank you, you're a star," said Cristine.

The road into the lodge was one way, so it wasn't a tough job; there would be no cars coming towards me and nothing I was likely to hit.

I pushed the seat back far enough to allow myself to get it and turned the key in the ignition. The car moved slowly forwards...excellent. I could remember what to do. This was all going to be fine. I drove forwards, heading towards the building that Cristine had asked me to park next to. But then, as I approached the building I saw a car coming towards me...it was going the wrong way down the one-way street.

I flashed my lights at it, waiting for the driver to reverse so I could go past, but he just flashed his lights back at me.

"Move over," I mouthed at him through the darkness. There was no way I was going to attempt to reverse back to where I started from, especially since he was in the wrong, I inched forward, but he inched forward too; I flashed him and he flashed back.

I had no idea what to do, I sat there for a while, then flashed him again but the guy just flashed me back. This was ridiculous.

Then there was a knock on my window, causing me practically to leap out of my seat.

I looked up to see Pieter standing there, confusion on his face. "What on earth are you doing?" he asked.

"I'm trying to work out why that guy won't reverse out of my way," I said. "I have the right of way; it's a one-way street for God's sake."

"What guy?" asked Pieter, looking genuinely surprised. "You're just sitting here, flashing your lights and beeping at no one."

I looked up to point at the vehicle ahead, and it was at that point that I realised the car ahead of me was exactly the same as mine...and there was a good reason for this – the car ahead was mine. What I'd been looking at was the reflection of my own vehicle in the mirrored outside of the building ahead of me.

"It doesn't matter, the car is gone now," I said, moving to drive the car forwards a little way and park it where Cristine had asked me to."

"You were looking at your car in the reflection on the building, weren't you?" said Pieter with a loud guffaw.

"Of course I wasn't," I said, winding the window up, and parking where Cristine had asked me. It was just a huge bloody relief that Dawn wasn't there to witness it.

I wandered back into the reception where Dawn was talking to Pieter. He turned to me as I walked in. "That is the funniest thing I've ever seen," he said, laughing uproariously, you just sitting there, flashing wildly at no one in particular and beeping your horn like a loony. So funny."

"Yeah, hysterical," I said. "Really funny."

I was excited to see where Pieter lived, not just because of a perfectly natural interest in anyone who's *that* good-looking, and an eagerness to find out more about him, but I was also genuinely interested in the lives the rangers led. On the surface they seemed to have such an attractive way of living - out in the wild all day with amazing animals, carrying a gun around and getting to feel like Crocodile Dundee, but I guessed there was a downside to the job, and it seemed most likely to me that the downside was that they didn't get paid very much and they didn't have great places to live.

"Here we are," said Pieter, as we pulled down a dirt track and came to a standstill outside what looked like an old shack. It was a miserable looking building - so different from the beauty of the lodge in which Dawn and I were staying. The fact that it was pitch black everywhere just made it all the more sinister-looking; so dark and isolated.

"Come on then." Pieter jumped down from the driving seat and moved towards the door. I scrabbled out in a way that I'd managed to adopt, stepping down onto the muddy ground and following Pieter to his front door. He kicked off his boots and put on the light, sending brightness over the sketchy furniture sitting in a rather dim and dirty looking room. It was the sort of furniture that gets thrown out by students, the sort of stuff that a charity shop in England would refuse to take.

"Have a seat," he said, and I perched on the desperately uncomfortable brown tweed sofa, reluctant to sit back for fear of never getting up again. The springs were definitely gone and it looked like the seat covers hadn't been washed since the 1960s.

"What do you fancy to eat?" said Pieter, walking into the kitchen.

"I don't mind." The truth was that I'd already eaten at the lodge, but if he was prepared to cook, then I'd happily eat a second dinner, just so we could sit romantically across from one another and break bread.

"It's not looking good, to be honest," he said, rummaging around inside a fridge which appeared to contain little except beer. "I've got nothing in here, food-wise, but a little bit of stale bread and some fruit the farmer gave me last week. It's looking a bit mouldy. I haven't even got any milk. I've got one beer, do you want half?"

"Oh," I said. "OK,"

I just assumed he would have gone shopping in advance of me coming over, and have some food prepared.

"I'm not much of a one for sorting out fancy dinners," he said, predicting my thoughts. "I tend to just live one day at a time."

It wasn't so much that he couldn't provide a fancy dinner, what was odd was that he couldn't even provide beans on toast...or beans on their own...or toast...or bread, or anything. Hell, the man couldn't even provide me with my own bottle of beer.

"Okay, well – should we go out somewhere?" he said.

"Is there a pub or anything like that nearby where we could go and grab a bite to eat?" I suggested.

"There is a cafe in the village. We could have a beer and a sandwich there," he said.

"Okay, let's do that. Then we can come back here and have a look at the cheetah stuff afterwards."

"Good plan," he said, grabbing the car keys and heading for the front door. I struggled my way out of the huge sofa, my knees buckling as I tried to stand up, and pulled my top down to make sure it was covering my stomach, before waddling after him and closing the door behind me. He seemed to leave the door open and not be at all concerned about who (or what!!) might enter in his absence. I'd have been terrified about what wildlife was going to call in while I was out.

He hitched me up into the Land Rover and we drove for about 10 minutes, into the local village, then he pulled over outside a small but cosy looking place. He had called it a cafe, but it was so lively that it was more like a Gastro pub or a small family-run restaurant. I could see through the small windows that there were table cloths and candles out everywhere, and really pretty flowers in the window boxes outside. My spirits lifted straight away.

"I love it when restaurants have white tablecloths," I said. "And candles. I always look for restaurants with tablecloths and candles."
Pieter looked at me as if I'd gone stark staring mad. "I'd never noticed that," he said. "I've been coming here for 17 years and I'd never noticed they had candles here. Women are mad."

"This is perfect," I said, clambering out of the Land Rover again in my effective but undignified way. I'd taken to rolling myself out, clinging onto the doorframe as I did so. Honestly, Land Rovers weren't designed for anyone over about 10 stone.

Pieter led the way into the cafe and I followed close behind. As soon as he swung the door open, the warmth of the atmosphere inside enveloped us. I could hear that a band was playing cover tunes and the waitresses smiled and said hello to Pieter, each of them drooling a little as he walked past him. He sat at a table which was clearly his regular and ordered two beers before I could say that I prefered wine. I looked up and the waitress had gone. It didn't matter – I'd drink beer and have wine next time.

"They do a great steak sandwich," he said. "It comes with chips.

"Great, that will do for me," I said, although I had imagined something a little more romantic... Perhaps some beautifully cooked seafood and a glass of chilled wine.

Pieter ordered our food and I leaned forward on my elbows and looked deep into his eyes.

"So, go on then, tell me everything you know about cheetahs."

But before Pieter could answer, we were interrupted by a small commotion as three very large, very drunk men came bundling over to our table.

"Hello matey, what we got here?" they said to Pieter.

When I looked at them more closely I realised it was three of the rangers.

"Pieter, my old man, so this is where you are. We been looking for you."

"This is Mary," said Pieter. "Do you know Marco, Liam and Steve?"

"No I don't. Nice to meet you," I said.

"Five beers," said Marco, waving his hand at the waitress. "Hang on, no - make it 10, no point messing around."

"Oh blimey. I think I'd prefer wine," I said, but my words were lost in the sound of chatter and cheering as the men downed their beers. This wasn't turning out to be quite the night I was hoping for.

"Come on, Mary, down in one."

I confess that I downed my beer, despite not really enjoying it, and knocked the next two back with equal gusto, just to keep up appearances. My food arrived and it was like a free-for-all, with everyone reaching in and grabbing chips. All that remained on the plate was a little garnish of lettuce and tomato...I nibbled at the edge of the tomato as the men chatted. They'd moved into talking Afrikaans which meant I was completely excluded. I don't think Pieter was doing it deliberately...it was just habit - beer and steak and a chat with the boys in their native tongue.

As the men chatted on, I looked around the pretty restaurant which had filled up considerably since we'd first arrived. To the right of us was a young, attractive couple and something about their body language drew me to them. I tuned into their conversation and soon realised they were debating whether or not to have an affair.

'I'm really attracted to you...' said the man.

"I'm attracted to you too," said the woman, more shyly.

It was captivating to listen. The man leaned over and took her hands and they just sat there staring at one another.

Another beer arrived on the table in front of me, distracting me momentarily. When I turned back to them a large man had entered the restaurant and was storming towards their table prompting them to quickly jump apart.

"Holy fuck," I said out loud. Pieter and his mates stopped their conversation and looked at me for the first time in about 20 minutes.

"What's the matter?" asked Pieter.

"It's about to kick off big time over there," I said. "Just watch."

By the time they all looked it was, indeed, all kicking off, with the husband having grabbed the affair guy round the neck. The woman started screaming for them to stop.

Pieter raced over to the fighting men, with his three musketeers in hot pursuit. I loved how much of an action man he was, how confident in his own abilities, how fearless. It was very alluring.

He arrived and easily separated the warring parties, much to the delight of the manager who told the warring duo to leave and sort out their issues elsewhere. By the time Pieter returned to the table, I was shaking a little...whether it was adrenalin, excitement or fear, I didn't know. Pieter wrapped my jacket around me.

"Come on, let's get you back," he said, leading me to the Land Rover and heaving me into it. "You can tell me what all that was about on the drive home."

CHAPTER ELEVEN

Dawn and I were up early and all ready for our penultimate day on safari. There was a sort of sadness as we got ready, knowing that so much of the holiday had already gone.

"I can't believe we fly home tomorrow night," said Dawn.

I couldn't either. I'd got so used to life here.

"I hope we see some amazing animals today," I said. "And I'd love to see the elephants close up again."

"And another kill," said Dawn. "I'd definitely like to see a load of lions kill something big right in front of us."

"OK," I said with a fake smile. "Yes, that would be lovely."

It's odd how the rhythm of a safari is something that starts to come naturally after just a couple of days. I don't feel traumatised by the early mornings like I did when we first arrived.

"Oh wow. I've got 600 new followers," said Dawn, lifting her head up from where it had been engrossed in her phone. "I was hoping to get 500 newbies in total so that's really good with a couple of days to go. Although, when I went to New York and bumped into Tom Cruise I gained about 10,000 followers as soon as I put the video on line."

"I guess me in a tree in my pants isn't quite as exciting as Tom Cruise," I said.

We went down to breakfast at 4am, me sweeping down the stairs, Hollywood style, as I'd taken to doing every time we went down. I found it impossible to descend them without pretending to be Marilyn Monroe in Gentlemen Prefer Blondes. I wished I'd brought a long red dress with me instead of just white and cream, then I could have done the staircase routine justice.

Breakfast was a quiet affair...Alexa and David had left the night before while I was out on my 'date' so there was only the four of us left. I regaled Patrick and Chris with tales of the couple from the restaurant the night before, and how manly and confident Pieter had been, then we set out on our morning adventure, heading down by the lake to watch the hippos. Cristine explained that when the hippos open their jaw right up and look like they are yawning, they are not yawning at all, but showing signs of being scared. She said as soon as we saw anything like that we would be backing away. I hoped the hippos would play ball and not do the mouth opening thing, because I really wanted to stay and watch them for as long as possible, they were such peculiar-looking creatures.

"It's been really lovely driving you lot around," Cristine said, suddenly, out of the blue. "Has it?" I asked, the surprise evident in my voice. I imagined she was fed up of us because we were a bit useless, but she said our enthusiasm has been a real joy.

"And you are keen to learn, that's been lovely," she said. "You seem really genuinely interested in knowing about the animals, not like some other people I've had to show around."

"Oh, do tell..." I said, dying to hear stories of really stupid people on Safari.

"Well, there was one time when a couple arrived at the wildlife reserve and the guy told one of the rangers that he wanted to propose to his girlfriend. He asked whether a giraffe could bring the ring to them while he was on one knee. It was baffling to all of us that he thought these wild animals could be made to perform circus tricks."

"Tell us more," I said.

Cristine laughed. "There was a couple from Germany who asked whether the animals got bored, and whether we couldn't bring out a TV for them so they could watch it during the day. They also asked whether the animals had access to a fridge."

We all laughed and smiled at one another, united in the warm glow of hearing that other people were much more stupid than we were.

Back in the lodge, I decided to have a shower before lunch. It had been so warm that morning I felt all hot and sticky. Also, the shower in the lodge was the stuff of fantasies so I tended to go in there quite a lot; there were all these settings that allowed you to have it raining on you, pouring on you, dripping on you or coming down at you with such ferocity that it almost bruised your scalp. I had tried the scalp bruising setting once and decided it wasn't for me. The other settings, though, were lovely. Rainwater was the best – a fine spray that tingled as it touched your skin – light and airy and very refreshing. I stepped out and wrapped a towel around my hair and around my body, padding into the bedroom to get dressed. Dawn was out on the balcony trying to look for hippos. She'd become utterly fascinated by them since Cristine told her they could run faster than Usain Bolt.

I slipped into my knickers and left the towel wrapped around me while I applied the lovely scented lotion that had been left in a straw basket in the bedroom. It was gorgeous – it smelled of everything lovely – like clouds and rainbows would smell if you could get close enough to sniff them.

I was aware of quite a commotion happening on the steps outside the room as I rubbed the lightly scented lotion into my thighs. It sounded as if there were loads of guys all jumping up and down. It was very odd. Then it all went quiet for a moment.

I popped my head out of the door but couldn't see anything. It was a beautiful sunny day and it was a lovely feeling when the sun's warm rays touched my skin, still slightly damp from the shower and lotion. I stood there awhile, enjoying the sensations.

But as I was enjoying the tingling of sunshine on skin, I noticed some movement in the bushes just in front of the steps to the apartment. It looked like a couple of people were there.

"Hello," I said. I had the sudden feeling it was Pieter. Perhaps he'd brought the cheetah stuff to show me after the disaster of last night. But why was he hiding in the bushes?

"Pieter," I tried. The figures stood still but didn't respond, it was the oddest thing. I walked slowly down the steps. "Pieter?"

I pushed my way into the bushes and that's when I saw them. It was two bloody baboons standing there. One squealed, the other just stared. I stood there, rooted to the spot, unsure what to do.

One of the baboons crouched down, turning his head slightly to one side and staring at me intently. The other baboon moved round so he was standing to the side of me. I had no idea what would make them go away. Perhaps if I threw something, they would turn to look at it and it would grant me a few minutes' grace in which I could escape back up the steps to the room. I moved to bend down but was terrified of taking my eyes off them. In any case, there was nothing to throw; nothing big enough to distract them. Then it occurred to me...there was only one thing for it...I removed the towel and hurled it with all my might. The baboons looked round as if flew through the air. I panicked and climbed up into the tree, screaming as loudly as I could as I went. Don't ask me why. Don't ask me why I didn't leg it back to the room. I guess my throwing of the towel was pretty feeble so the baboons weren't distracted for long; I didn't think I'd make it back there in time. So there I was - once again up a tree in order to escape from an animal that was perfectly able to get into the tree should it want to.

The baboons were screeching up at me and I was screaming for help. We were making a tremendous amount of noise, someone had to hear us soon, surely.

In the distance I saw the sight of khaki green shirts running towards me. Thank God. It was Marco, Liam and Steve, the guys I'd met in the pub with Pieter.

"Here," I shouted, waving hysterically.

The baboons shrieked louder and one, then the other, jumped up into the tree next to me.

By the time the rangers arrived all three of us were in the tree, sitting on the lowest branch, me covering my breasts with my hands, them looking at me quizzically. We'd only been there only a couple of minutes, but they had shuffled over so close that we were all sitting next to one another, like we were waiting for a bus or something.

Unbeknownst to me, Dawn, the intrepid blogger had witnessed the whole episode. She had seen the drama unfold and heard the screams and had done what a reliable blogger will always do in such circumstances – she'd filmed it all. With scant regard for Mary's feelings and no regard for her privacy, she'd shown the world the picture of Mary half naked in a tree with two baboons. Then, when gun-toting rangers had arrived, she had filmed that too, finishing her recording with the sight of Mary's larger than average bottom descending. She marked it 'Fat Girl stuck in tree: Part Two. This time with added baboons!' and loaded it onto the blog.

CHAPTER TWELVE

After everything that had happened during the day, the last thing I wanted to do in the evening was to go out drinking. I felt drained. It had taken four rangers to rescue me, and once again Dawn had captured it on video. When I spoke to her about it she gave me a huge hug and said she loved me and she was sorry if I was offended. Offended? Try humiliated. The damn thing had been trending on Twitter all afternoon and she now had 10,000 more followers. I'd matched Tom Cruise...or, more likely, the screaming baboons had matched Tom Cruise.

It was all bloody exhausting. I just wanted to curl up on the bed, watch some terrible South African television, and get lots of sleep. Tomorrow was the last day and we were doing something called 'walk on the wild side' in the morning where we'd go out on foot to get closer to the animals and see more of the insects and plant life. I knew I'd enjoy it much more if I did it without a hangover.

I slipped on my pyjamas, tied my hair back from my face, and prepared to relax for the evening.

I pulled back the sheets and climbed in. I curled up into a little ball and found myself thinking about Ted. The holiday had taught me lots of things, and one of them was that Ted was a really good guy, and I should be making more of an effort to make our relationship work. He was worth sticking with, even when things weren't perfect. He was one of life's good guys.

As I was lying there, lost in my thoughts, I suddenly felt water on my legs. I put my hand down and could feel that my pyjama bottoms were soaked.

Oh my God – I'd wet myself, this was a nightmare.

I leaped out of bed, my pyjama trousers wet through, and went to head for the bathroom, but before I could get there, there was a knock on the door. It must Dawn; probably come back to check I was OK. We had been leaving the door ajar so that neither of us needed to take out keys with us, but tonight I'd closed it firmly against the world, fearful of baboons and the looks of pity from everyone who'd seen the video.

But, when I swung the door open, it was Pieter who was standing there, clutching a carrier bag in one hand and two bottles of wine in the other.

"I thought you might be feeling low. I wanted to cheer you up," he said.

I stood in front of him, my 19 stone body encased in unflattering, too-tight pyjamas, having wet myself minutes earlier, my hair was scraped back off my face. It's possible that no one in the world had ever looked worse. I smiled at him.

"I wasn't expecting guests," I said.

"Clearly," he said, smiling back.

Then we both burst out laughing, and I swung open the door.

"Come in," I said.

"Look, I saw what happened today and the blog and everything and I wanted to check you were OK. He wandered over and sat on the edge of the bed. The bed in which the sheets were soaking wet from me having peed myself. To say it was mortifying was a gross understatement.

"Why don't we sit on the balcony," I said, opening the French windows and trying to tempt him away from the wet bed.

"Oh no," he said, spotting the damp sheets. "Did it break?"

"Did what break?"

"I asked house-keeping to put heated water bottle in the bed to warm it up for you. Looks like it's leaked everywhere."

"Oh thank God," I said, abandoning all efforts at decorum. "I thought I'd wet myself."

"You thought what?"

"Really - I thought I'd wet myself. That's why I was trying to get you to come outside...to get you away from the sheets."

"You're mad," said Pieter, pulling out a broken hot water bottle from the bed before following me towards the French windows. "I'm happy to sit outside, but won't you get cold out here in just your pyjamas?"

We compromised by bringing the duvets out and wrapping them round us while we sat and drank wine and dunked crisps into hummus.

"This is great," I told him. "I'm so glad you came over."

"I'm glad too," he said, squeezing my hand, leading me to drop a chunk of pitta bread into the dip.

"You know - if I'd realised that Dawn had been filming everything I'd definitely have said something to try to stop her," said Pieter. "None of us knew she was doing it. She's very sneaky. I think she's behaved appallingly. I told her just now."

"Did you? I didn't feel like I could make a massive fuss

because she's the one who got me this holiday, and it was always stated that the point of the trip was to write the blog."

"Yes, but not like this," said Pieter. "I think she's been incredibly cruel."

"Thanks," I said. It felt good to know that he was on my side.

"Anyway – I told her she owes you big time, and she's promised to look after you in future and not stitch you up."

"Thanks," I said again, giving him a small hug. As Pieter spoke, I could hear my phone ringing in the room...it was coming from somewhere deep in the tangled, wet sheets. I decided to leave it. It was probably Dawn, ringing to apologise after her chat with Pieter.

"More wine," he said.

"Thank you," I replied. "This is so lovely."

Ted pushed his phone into his pocket and sat back into the seat at Johannesburg airport. He'd wanted to let Mary know he was turning up. He didn't want just to appear unannounced at her door. He had phoned ahead to the safari place to tell them he was coming, but he had no idea whether Henrique, the guy he'd spoken to, was actually going to let him in when he arrived. He'd tried Mary several times but she just wasn't answering her phone. He'd have to work it all out when he arrived. He would touch down in Cape Town at midnight, so should be with her by around 3am. Presumably she'd be tucked up in bed at that time, and he could burst in and give her a lovely surprise.

"Tell me some of the silliest things that have happened while you've been working as a ranger," I said, as I pulled the duvet over my shoulders and looked out into the sky, full of the brightest stars I'd ever seen. The lack of light pollution made them quite dazzling.

"Oh, I've seen everything," said Pieter. "I've had baboons open car doors and get in. Just once, but it was quite a shock for these four women sitting in the back. I had to jump over the seats and clamber into the back to shoo them out. They went pretty quickly, but it was all a bit alarming to start with."

"Did they leave the door open or something?" I asked.

"No, but you used to be able to open the doors from the outside...you can't any more because of incidents like that."

"What's the worst thing people do?"

"I guess it's two things – the first is to ask really stupid questions, the second is to be too brightly coloured and too noisy."

"Oooo..so even though I looked like I'd stepped out of the Victorian era, I was OK with my beige palette of clothing then?"

"You were perfect," he said. "It's the multiple neon colors that tend to cause the problems. And the noise that people make, honestly - when you've been out on a game-drive for over two hours, searching an area where there was a recent leopard sighting, everybody is craning their necks, looking in all directions to get a glimpse of the animal, then - suddenly - the bloke in the row behind you bellows "LEOPARD OVER THERE" at the top of his voice. You swivel round and if you're lucky you'll glimpse a tail disappearing."

"Oh God, that would be a real pain," I said.

As Pieter picked up the bottle to refill my glass, I noticed that one of his fingers was shorter than the other. It looked as if the end had been cut off.

"What happened to your finger?" I asked.

"Ah," he replied. "That was the time I got too close to a lion. I was trying to pull a thorn out of it's foot. I gently held its paw in my hands but he turned and bit the end of my finger off."

"Oh no! That's awful. It must have been bloody agony. And you're miles from a hospital here. Where on earth did they take you? What did they do?"

"Nothing. I decided it would be OK, so for a few days I didn't get any treatment at all...I just hung out here with my finger all wrapped up, then I started to feel faint and shivery and we thought I'd better seek treatment. By the time I did, the end of my finger was completely hanging off and couldn't be saved."

"Jesus Christ. You were lucky not to lose your whole arm."

"I was lucky not to die, to be honest. A weaker person would definitely have been killed by the lion on that day." He looked so solemn as he spoke, then he smiled from ear-to-ear. "I'm sorry. That's a load of bollocks," he said. "There was no lion. I got completely hammered in the pub and cut it on a pane of glass."

"You rotter!" I said. "But, for the record, the first story's much better. Stick to that.

I looked at my watch. It was 1am already. How had it got that late? Dawn must have come in and gone to bed, leaving us out on the balcony chatting away.

"Are you warm enough?" asked Pieter.

"To be honest, I'm starting to feel a bit chilly," I said.

"Come on, let's go inside."

I followed Pieter into the room where it was much warmer. We'd finished one bottle of wine, so Pieter grabbed the other one, and the remainder of the food, and we sat on the soft carpet, leaning back against the bed, with our mini picnic laid out in front of us.

"Can a kangaroo jump higher than the Empire State Building?" I asked.

Pieter looked at me expectantly. "I don't know, Mary," he replied.

"Of course," I said. "The Empire State Building can't jump."

"Yep. That's the sort of standard I've come to expect from you, Mary Brown."

"OK - another one. What did the elephant say to the naked man?"

"I don't know, but I dread to think," said Pieter.

"How do you breathe through something so small?"

"Oh dear. These are getting much worse. I'm going to need more wine if we're going to carry on like that. Want a top up?"

"Yeah," I said, enthusiastically, even though I'd already had way more than I was planning to. I'd been determined to go to bed early and sober. Now I was at the stage where I couldn't be bothered to worry about it any more, I felt invincible, as if I could drink as much as I wanted and all would be fine.

"Why couldn't the leopard play hide and seek?" I said.

"Go on..."

"Because he was always spotted."

Dawn lay in bed, listening to the chatter from Mary's room. She was glad that Pieter and Mary were getting on so well. She felt a bit bad about always videoing Mary and putting it up on the blog, but that's what she did. That's why she was here. That was her job. If she stopped putting funny videos on the blog, people wouldn't look at it, and the lovely life she'd built for herself, through her blogging, would be over in a heartbeat. She'd always done this when she'd been on holiday, it was just that she'd never been on holiday with someone quite like Mary before...someone who was forever getting herself into stupid scrapes.

She giggled to herself as she thought of Mary stuck in the tree. And to do it twice! It really was the funniest thing. She could see why it had so many hits and had been bouncing around on social media all afternoon.

CHAPTER THIRTEEN

"I've really enjoyed being here with you," said Pieter, giving me a friendly squeeze of the shoulder.

"Me too," I said. "You're really good company Pieter."

"Thanks," he replied. "I wish all women thought that...I seem to have absolutely no luck at all with the opposite sex."

"Whaaaaat?" I asked. "I mean – really? I don't believe that for a second."

"It's true," he said. "There's this girl I really like, but I just don't think she's at all interested in me."

"What girl – tell me everything," I said.

"No, I can't."

"Well, if you don't tell me, I can't help you, can I? In any case, I'm going home tomorrow night – it's not as if I can do much damage between now and then."

Pieter raised his eyebrows and looked at me askance. "Not a day has gone by since you've been here when you haven't caused a whole pile of damage, Mary Brown. You're very loveable but chaos does seem to follow you around the place."

"I can't argue with that," I said, nodding wisely. "But I'm always chaotic and disruptive to myself. I'd never do anything to hurt anyone else. Not ever."

"I know, I know," he said. "I realise that. That's why I came round tonight – because when I saw the video of you online I knew that you would never have done the same to Dawn. I remember how you deliberately didn't video her when she screamed at the cheetah. You're a lovely person."

"Well, if I'm so lovely you can tell me. Come on Crocodile Dundee – spill the goss..."

"OK," he said, laughing at me. "I really like Cristine, but I just don't think she's interested in me."

"Cristine?" I said. "Really?"

"Yes, why do you look so surprised?"

"Because I had no idea."

"Didn't you? But, I've been really obvious. Rushing to help her out when she calls – only to find you stuck up a tree, helping her with all the oil barrels last night."

"That's not obvious at all," I cried. "You really need to make it much more obvious. I bet she doesn't have a clue."

"Oh God – I hate all this," he said. "I wish I'd never told you now."

"Why do you wish you'd never told me? I can help," I said.

"The thing I want to know is whether she likes me," he said. I had to stop myself from explaining to him that every woman in the whole damn world probably fancied him.

"I'll find out," I said. "Leave it with me. I'll be subtle, I promise."

"Thank you, you're wonderful," he said, giving me a huge hug. It was a lovely big warm embrace, but it was just friendly, there was no sense of romance or sexual interest... Just two people who had spent a lovely night chatting to one another and had become firm friends.

"I think you're pretty wonderful too," I said, and he pulled me even closer to him.

As we sat in the lovely warm embrace, bonded by a mutual respect and a great friendship, the door suddenly burst open and Dawn rushed in, her hair standing up on end and a look of utter horror on her face.

"Ted's here," she screamed. "The security guards just phoned through to say he's here. Pieter – you'd better hide, quick."

I looked up as Pieter disengaged himself from our warm embrace and threw himself under the bed. As he did, there was a loud knock on the door.

"God, he's here already," I said, running to the door and opening it cautiously.

"Hello my beautiful angel," said Ted, wrapping his arms around me. "God I've missed you. I just couldn't stay away any more... I wanted to see you to check you were okay."

"I'm absolutely fine," I said, my voice loud and high-pitched and shot through with panic.

"What's the matter?" he said. "You sound really worried."

"No no," I said. "I'm just excited. It's so wonderful to see you."

"I'll leave you to to it," said Dawn, backing out of the room, and giving me a look which said 'Pieter's under the bed, your boyfriend has just arrived at the door, I don't know what to do, so I'll just get out of here".

Ted looked up as Dawn left, closing the door behind her. "I haven't seen you all week, you gorgeous woman. You look amazing..." As he spoke, he lifted my arms into the air and removed my pyjama top, pushing me back towards the bed.

"Why don't we go and get some breakfast or something?" I said.

"Let's have breakfast later," he said.

He took his shirt off and began unzipping his trousers as he pushed me back onto the bed. He began kissing me passionately and urgently. I hadn't been to bed all night, I was half-drunk and starting to feel exhausted, and now we were going to make love in a bed on top of Pieter. To say this holiday had descended into farce would be to totally underplay the madness of it all.

"You know I love you don't you," said Ted. "Now let me put my hand on your little muffin."

He pushed me back onto the bed, and I swear to God I heard a squeal from beneath us. While Ted continued to talk about my little muffin – his embarrassing pet name for my most private of parts, he kissed me more passionately, removing all our clothes and beginning to breathe heavily and tell me how excited he was. All I could think about was Pieter lying under the bed. Ted pushed himself inside me and I could feel the bed move and push against the wall. Neither Ted nor I was small; I was well aware that the bed would be pushing down on top of Pieter as he lay beneath the springs. Ted began moaning and pushing harder and the bed rocked even more. Oh God, this was unbearable. Finally Ted rose to a climax and grunted, roared and squealed in delight. There was no way I was going to orgasm with Pieter under the bed, so when Ted continued to touch me, trying to rise me, I pushed his arm away and held him in a warm embrace. "Just cuddle me," I pleaded.

"Are you sure, is everything okay?" he said.

"Everything is lovely," I said. "I'm so glad you are here, but I'm really hungry, let's go and get some breakfast. They have the best breakfast buffet here – it's brilliant. It's open from 2am for those going out on early safaris."

"Okay then," said Ted. He jumped out of bed and dressed and the two of us left the room and walked down to the buffet bar.

Around 10 minutes later Pieter came wandering through the restaurant and said hello, introducing himself to Ted.

"You must speak nothing of what happened just then," I said threateningly, when Ted had set off on a second trip to the buffet.

Pieter smiled broadly at me.

"Okay," he said. "You can rely on me... my little muffin."

CHAPTER FOURTEEN

Neither of us had slept the night before but the walking safari was one of the highlights of the week, so I really didn't want to miss it. Pieter said that it was no problem for Ted to come with us, so we headed off on the Land Rover together, with Chris, Patrick and Dawn sitting on the seats behind us. I could sense that Dawn wasn't happy about Ted being there. She wasn't terribly happy that I had a boyfriend, I don't suppose, though I was very glad that she had burst in last night to tell me he was on the way.

We had both Cristine and Pieter with us for the walking safari because you're not allowed to wander around out of the Land Rover with just one ranger to guide you. I knew that I needed to get Cristine on her own so I could find out how she felt about Pieter. After having sex on top of him this morning, that felt like the least I could do.

"Wow, look, elephants," said Ted. "This is bloody amazing. It's like Jurassic Park."

Ted's enthusiasm for the animals reminded me of my own enthusiasm on the first day. I'd kind of got used to them being around every corner now, but Ted was wide-eyed as he watched them.

"A baby elephant," he squealed. "Look."

"Shall we get out and go closer?" said Pieter.

He looked over at Cristine who nodded and smiled. I knew in that instant that she liked him...it was so bloody obvious. Why hadn't I realised that before? Why couldn't he see that?

We all stepped out of the Land Rover. Ted helped me down so I didn't have to do my bizarre rolling routine, and we walked carefully towards the elephants. Honestly, it was the most amazing experience of my life. Cristine led the way given she was queen of the elephants and told Ted all about what emotional creatures they were and how she'd seen them cry and respond with real tenderness to their young.

I held back so I was walking with Pieter.

"Everything OK?" he asked.

"Fine," I said. "I'm sure that Cristine likes you."

"She does? How on earth would you know that?"

"I just do...feminine intuition. I can tell. You have to ask her out."

"No way," said Pieter.

"But – why?"

"Because...I don't know, just because..."

"Just say to her 'do you fancy going out for a glass of wine tonight?' Just say it."

"Oh God," said Pieter, looking nervous at the thought of it. It was a very sweet moment; this big, strong man with his huge shoulders and massive boots, clutching a gun and looking terrifying, but as nervous as hell about asking a pretty girl out on a date. I'd seen him charge in to break up a huge fight without a care in the world, but the idea of asking someone out had left him crippled with nerves.

"Maybe later," he said.

We caught up with the others, and Ted was entertaining Cristine with his collection of terrible jokes.

"There was a Mummy Mole, a Daddy Mole and a Baby Mole. They lived in a hole out in the country near a farmhouse. Dad poked his head out of the hole and said, "Mmmm, I smell sausage!" Mum mole poked her head outside the hole and said, "Mmmm, I smell pancakes!" Baby mole tried to stick his head outside but couldn't because of the two bigger moles. Baby mole said, "The only thing I smell is molasses. Get it? Mole arses... see!"

"Blimey, that's truly awful," said Pieter. "You and Mary were definitely made for one another – both your jokes are appalling."

"Oy," I said, prodding him in the side. "Go and talk to Cristine."

"OK," he said, terror written on his face. "I'll go and talk to her now."

The walk on the wild side was great fun...we saw tortoises, birds, flowers and plants as well as the elephants. We even found some rhino that we tracked from a distance.

"We have to come back here," said Ted, when we were back in the room and packing for our flight home. "Shall we start a blog or something...one fat couple? It might work."

"Ha!" I said, noncommittally. I'd loved the holiday but I honestly think I might have had enough of blogs for now.

Ted and I sat together on the flight home...in economy, of course, while Dawn trundled up to business class with a huge grin on her face. I guess the whole thing had been a giant success for her; some brilliant, compelling videos on the site, and loads more people signed up. Presumably that would mean lots more free trips for her and more income from advertisers. The woman was a pain in the arse but you had to admire her in many ways.

"All things considered, and bearing in mind that the whole world has seen your bottom, would you ever consider going on holiday with Dawn again?"

"No," I said.

"Even if it was a free trip to somewhere really exotic?"

"No," I said with a shrug. "It's quite simple, Ted, I've realised that free trips and luxury and exotic surroundings and all that are wonderful when you're with someone you love. Not so great when you're with a complete nutcase. Having said that, I met some amazing friends – Pieter was great wasn't it?"

"Yes, he was," conceded Ted. "He's a nice guy, bit too good looking for my tastes, though."

Ted nudged me in an affectionate way as he said this.

"It must've been horrifying to be at home and see all those ridiculous videos appearing on the blog," I said.

"It was insane," said Ted. "I made the mistake of telling my mum and sister all about the blog so they've been looking at it too. My sister wants to know where you got those lacy knickers from."

"Oh God, this is all getting worse by the minute," I said. "Dawn's nuts"

"Yep, she does seem to be. Do you think you'll stay in touch with her at all?"

"I don't think so, but then I didn't think I would stay in touch after bumping into each other in the garden centre, and we ended up on safari in Africa together, so you never know. I was thinking I should get her a nice present to say thank you. I know she only invited me because I'm fat, but it was a hell of a trip in the end, wasn't it? An amazing experience, and such an incredibly beautiful place. I'll just make sure I don't go on holiday with her again."

The air hostess appeared beside Ted and asked us to turn our phones off and put our tray tables up in advance of the flight taking off.

I checked my phone one last time. I had a text...from Pieter.

"Hey blondie – just wanted to say thanks for making the past week more memorable than any other week I've ever had. You're a very special lady...don't let anyone ever tell you otherwise. Pieter x PS I'm taking Cristine out for dinner tonight."

Yes. Brilliant.

As I was about to turn the phone off, another text popped across the screen. It was from Dawn.

"I've been invited on a cruise in three weeks' time," it said. "Do you want to come?"

Oooooo...a cruise. I looked over at Ted who was engrossed in his phone. I couldn't could I? But then again...

"I'd love to," I texted back. "Count me in."

I switched off my phone and put it away.

"Everything OK?" asked Ted. "You look thoughtful."

"Everything's fine," I said. "I've got one little thing to tell you, but let's get you a nice large gin and tonic first..."

If you enjoyed the book, why not try Cruise with an Adorable Fat Girl, available now:

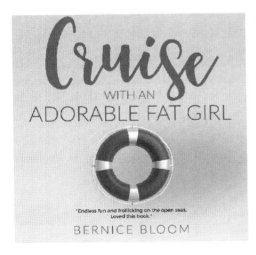

Mary Brown - our full-figured heroine - is off on a cruise. It's the trip of a lifetime...featuring eat-all-you-can buffets and a trek through Europe with a 96-year-old widower called Frank and a flamboyant Spanish dancer called Juan Pedro. Then there's the desperately handsome captain, the appearance of an ex-boyfriend on the ship, the time she's mistaken for a Hollywood film star in Lisbon and tonnes of clothes shopping all over Europe.

See www.bernicebloom.com for all the books in the Adorable Fat Girl series

Printed in Great Britain
by Amazon

59509459R00078